Glitter

Glitter

Eliza Grace Howard

ARCHWAY PUBLISHING

Archway Publishing books may be ordered through booksellers or by contacting:

Archway Publishing
1663 Liberty Drive
Bloomington, IN 47403
www.archwaypublishing.com
844-669-3957

ISBN: 978-1-6657-4773-8 (sc)
ISBN: 978-1-6657-4775-2 (hc)
ISBN: 978-1-6657-4774-5 (e)

Library of Congress Control Number: 2023914242

Print information available on the last page.

Archway Publishing rev. date: 9/22/2023

Chapter One

Becky set the cheap suitcase down on the concrete surface of the street and straightened, her eyes fixed on the small house across the street. In the near darkness, where the only illumination was from a streetlight fifty feet or so down the street on the far side of the next house, the house looked forlorn and somewhat unkempt. The windows were dark, and the front lawn looked in need of mowing behind the short picket fence along the front, which was more decorative than useful; the plantings bordering the fence inside the yard were tall and ungainly. The short gravel driveway on the right side of the property, which led up from the street, was empty.

Her eyes burned for a moment. It could have been today or fifteen years ago. Nothing looked the least bit different.

Becky's hand moved to the small of her back, and she rubbed it absently as she stared intently at the house. After a moment, she picked up the suitcase and walked a few feet farther down her side of the street to where a large tree grew close to the pavement. There were no sidewalks here on Pine Street, not in this tiny North Carolina town. Geographically, this was probably near the center of town but certainly not the most affluent area. Here the houses were small, the owners too financially insignificant to rate this amenity.

The late September air was cool and pleasant; no breeze was

stirring, and there was just a hint of fall in the hushed atmosphere. She set her burden down, and her knees folded as she slowly sank down to sit at the base of the tree, leaning back against the trunk for support. She waited.

Not long afterward, a vehicle approached the house from down the street on her right, its headlights briefly illuminating the yard and front porch of the house as it turned up the short driveway and stopped at the side of the house.

Becky's drooping eyes flew open, and she sat still, watching, as the driver-side door opened. The interior light illuminated the slim figure of a woman as she emerged, reached back inside the vehicle to retrieve a tote bag, then straightened and approached the house, pausing at a side doorway and seconds later disappearing inside. A light came on, spilling out through both the doorway and a window near the back of the house. The door swung closed, eliminating the spill of light into the yard. Minutes later, a glow showed through the front windows as more lights came on in the depths of the house.

Across the street, Becky got to her feet, picked up her suitcase, and walked unhurriedly across the pavement toward the house. She bent over to unlatch the gate in the center of the short picket fence in front and let herself into the yard. She walked up the narrow gravel walk that bisected the yard, headed up a pair of concrete steps, and crossed the wooden planks of the porch.

The front entrance was covered by a screen door hinged in front of the sturdy wood one with twin panes of glass set too high to see through. A pull on the screen door's handle proved it to be latched shut, so Becky raised her fist and rapped loudly on the plank frame of the screen door. She had just raised her arm to knock a second time when she heard approaching footsteps; she blinked as the porch was bathed in sudden dazzling light from an overhead fixture in the porch ceiling behind her. The wood inner door was yanked open, and the woman who had been driving the car stood there, staring out at her visitor. Her eyes widened in recognition, and her mouth went slightly agape.

"What are you doing here?" she rasped.

Becky smiled at her through the screen barrier. "Now what kind of greeting is that for your long-lost sister?" she said. "Hello, Clara."

The surprise on Clara's face gave way to a frown. "I asked you what you want."

"I want to come in the house, for one thing," Becky said flatly. "It's been a long day, I've come a far distance, and I'm tired. Are you going to let me come in?"

There was a long, intense moment as the pair stared at each other; the woman inside moved her hand, and a click indicated she had unlatched the screen door. She stepped backward without saying a word.

Becky pulled open the screen door and walked inside past her sister. Her eyes darted around the small alcove just inside the doorway and past it to a small room on the right, furnished with a well-worn sofa and a matching pair of armchairs. A small, round table stood at either end of the sofa, each holding a lamp and a few pieces of bric-a-brac, and a low, wooden coffee table sat in front of it. Becky knew that a small TV set sat out of sight of the doorway on a metal stand on the opposite wall, and an oval braided rug covered the middle half of the oak floor. The sight and familiar smell of the house hit her like a blow to the midsection.

"It looks just like I remember," she said softly.

"What did you expect?" Her sister pushed the front door shut behind her, threw the lock, and switched off the porch light. "Did you think I was going to redecorate?"

"Clara, I …"

"What are you doing here, Becky?"

Becky set her suitcase down. Her hand went to her forehead, and her lean fingers massaged the space between her brows. "Would you believe me if I said I don't honestly know?"

"Well, if you're looking for another handout, you're at the wrong place." Clara moved to face her, slimmer and a few inches shorter, the stern lines of her face making her look a decade older. "I'm barely making ends meet. I ain't got no extra money to give you for you to snort up your nose!"

Becky's hand dropped. "I'm not into that anymore," she protested. "I've been clean for nearly two years now."

"Well, good for you, if you're telling the truth!"

"I am. I swear I am."

They stared at each other for a long moment. Clara was the first to yield. "You want something to drink?" she asked, dropping her gaze. "The only thing I got is cold water or sodas."

"Water sounds fine. Yeah, I'd appreciate a drink of water."

They walked slowly toward the back of the house and into the kitchen. Becky pulled out a high-backed chair at the kitchen table and sank onto it as Clara opened the old, round-shouldered refrigerator door and delved around inside it, lifting out a half-gallon mason jar filled with a clear liquid. She took a glass from a cabinet and poured it almost full, handing it to her sister.

"How'd you get here?" Clara asked.

"Bus from Nashville to Winston-Salem. Hitchhiked the rest of the way here to Phillips. Walked here from the highway after the randy ol' coot I was riding with let me out of his pickup over by the shopping center." Becky took the glass and gulped thirstily.

Clara took a deep breath. "You hungry?"

"What you got?"

"I dunno—some leftover mac and cheese, I think. I got eggs if you wanna cook them. I think there's a tomato."

"I'll take the tomato."

"Still watching your figure?" Clara's voice dripped with sarcasm.

"Yeah. As a matter of fact, I am."

The women glared at each other for a moment before Clara spoke. "Well, I've got to go take a shower and get to bed. I been on my feet since five o'clock this morning, worked about a shift an' a half, and I gotta be back there again at five in the morning. I guess you're planning on spending the night. The bed's made up in Mama's old room. You can sleep there." She turned to leave the room.

"Clara …" Becky paused and looked back over her shoulder. "Thank you," she barely whispered, clutched the glass, and looked entreatingly at her sister.

Clara didn't respond. She sailed on out of the room as Becky got up, seized the tomato out of the refrigerator, and took it over to the sink. She didn't look for a knife but bit hungrily into it, licking the juice from her fingers as she ate. She could hear a shower running somewhere back in the house. When it stopped, Becky walked back through the house and retrieved her suitcase from where she had set it down near the front door.

She made her way to the second bedroom; she could have walked through the house blindfolded. She switched on a small lamp on the bedside table, and her muscles slumped as she looked around her. The room seemed totally unchanged from how she remembered it, and she could almost see the small woman lying propped up under the white chenille bedspread, her raven hair shot with gray strands spread out across the pillow, her face drawn and pale.

"Mama," she whispered as tears momentarily blinded her. Impatiently, she swiped at them with a fist. Moving rapidly, she stripped off her clothes and dropped them in a pile on the floor beside the bed. She turned down the covers and slid between the sheets. The last sound she was conscious of was the click as she reached up and turned off the lamp, her head settling back on the pillow.

Clara's eyes popped open; the light outside her bedroom windows was still gray, but this was the hour when she awoke every morning of her life. But something didn't feel right this morning. The house was dark and still, but something just seemed off to her. Then she remembered. She wasn't alone in her little house; her sister, Becky, was here, sleeping in the other bedroom.

Becky! Clara closed her eyes, voices from the past filling her head. *Oh, look at Becky! She's the beauty in that family! Too bad her sister's so plain. Did you hear Becky sing that solo in church this morning? What a voice that child has! Poor little Clara, stuck here and taking care of her mama while that Becky's off, becoming a famous singer!*

And there were the other comments, too, made even more quietly behind a sheltering hand to the mouth: *It's a no wonder her mama's sick in bed with that wild child of hers! That Becky of hers is going to worry that poor woman to death.* But Clara still had heard them, those asides she wasn't supposed to. She sighed.

Becky was still beautiful … all that long, auburn hair cascading down her back, her face still smooth, maybe just a hint of lines beside her mouth, her eyes still wide and expressive. But without any signs of crows-feet suggesting she was no longer twenty, she was the prettiest girl in Phillips.

Clara got out of bed and put on a freshly ironed uniform. She'd never minded—at least not too much anyway—that she was the responsible one, the one her mama had depended on to take care of the house, see that the bills were paid, and make sure Mama got to her numerous doctor appointments. She had loved her mama, letting her constant complaining and demands slide right off her like water off a duck's back.

Being a caregiver had been hard; Clara certainly knew that. It had been a tiring, thankless, never-ending task, but if she hadn't done it, who would have? What she resented was the blind spot Mama had always had where Becky was concerned. No matter what Becky did—no matter what kind of scrape she got herself into—Mama would just smile and let it go. Clara had tried so hard to please—all As in school, honor roll, Beta Club—but nothing she had done seemed to matter as much as Becky's getting to be class attendant or riding out onto the football field on the back of a convertible in her prom dress during halftime of the homecoming football game.

She wasn't jealous, Clara told herself as she jerked the shoelaces on her comfortable work shoes and tied them. Mama was gone now, and she had done her duty and taken care of her, right up to the very end. She had nothing to regret. So, what if Becky had broken every rule and skipped through life, doing exactly what Becky wanted to do without a single thought about the consequences she had left scattered in her wake? Becky had always been the golden one, the talented one, pursuing a life of fame and glitter. Even now, she was still her little sister, all the close family she had left.

Clara crept quietly to the closed bedroom door, cracked it, and peeked in. A shape rested quietly under the covers; her sister was sleeping soundly. Clara closed the door and hurried out to her car.

The little town's streets were almost empty at this hour. Everything looked as calm and peaceful as night, surrendered to the first rays of the rising sun. Clara parked her old car behind the diner and hurried up to the back door. A light was shining out from the kitchen, where Miss Carrie, the black lady who was the morning cook, was already hard at work, mixing and kneading the dough for the several dozen homemade-from-scratch biscuits she made six days a week, which the breakfast crowd, soon to start drifting in, would quickly consume.

"Good morning, Miss Carrie," Clara said as she came in and went straight to the big coffee pot to start the first batch brewing.

"Morning, Clara," said Miss Carrie, her flour-covered hands deep in the pan of dough, a big smile lighting her dark face. Together they fell into their familiar routine of getting ready for the daily opening.

Sunlight was pouring in through the lace curtains when Becky opened her eyes. The house was absolutely quiet except for the occasional creak or pop old houses make. Becky sat up and looked around, momentarily disoriented. As realization poured over her, she swung her legs off the bed and stood, looking around her, and the years slipped away.

Mama's prized wicker dressing table sat in the corner near the double windows, some of her perfume bottles still sitting on it. Becky smiled; Arpege, Channel No. 5, Norrell—how Mama had prized her small collection, sparingly dabbing some on for only the most special of occasions. And special occasions were few and far between for her.

Becky's mouth tightened, and she walked out of the room naked and headed toward the kitchen. After plundering through the cabinets, she managed to find the coffee tin and a small pan, which she filled halfway with water and added two eggs to boil.

Half an hour later, with some protein in her belly and a second mug of coffee in hand, Becky began to feel half human. A nice, long, hot shower was in order, she decided. Then she'd have to start figuring out what she was going to do. Already, the silence in this place was starting to press down on her; she was going to have to make a plan. She headed toward the only bathroom in the house and started the shower water running.

After a leisurely time under the hot running water, Becky wrapped a towel around her hair, returned to the bedroom, and began pulling clothes out of her suitcase, eyeing each garment critically before tossing it down on top of her unmade bed. She settled on a low-cut knit top over a maxi skirt. She frowned as she sat and laced up her well-worn sneakers. Definitely a jarring note, not in keeping with the image she was going for, but maybe whoever it was wouldn't be looking at her feet, and there was no way to get to where she was going without some walking. Her first priority was to get some wheels.

Going back into the bathroom, she plugged in her blow-dryer and spent the next hour making her hair cascade down to the tops of her shoulder blades in a spill of thick, auburn waves. Next, she carefully applied her makeup—not too much; this town called for a light touch—including eyeliner and mascara to widen and deepen her hazel eyes. She added lip liner and a lot of gloss to make her lips all pouty and sexy. She peered into the steamy mirror over the sink and nodded with satisfaction.

"Okay, showtime!" she murmured to herself.

Grabbing her purse, she removed the few bills she had left, folded them, and inserted them in her bra, just under the low neckline of her top. Leaving the house, she began her hike down the street, headed toward downtown Phillips. At the end of Pine Street, she turned onto a much busier street—a two-lane highway that slowed as it ran through town—watching the traffic carefully to catch a ride.

Becky pulled open the car door and hopped out onto the sidewalk just outside the Ford dealership on Main Street. She gave the driver a lingering look. "Thank you so much. You don't know how much I appreciate the lift," she told him. She slammed the door halfway into his "My pleasure, ma'am" and immediately turned her attention to her next objective.

She took in the big, modern-looking building with its sleek glass front showcasing the current-model vehicles parked inside as she made her way down the sidewalk to where Main Street cornered with a side street running alongside the dealership.

She headed toward the used car lot set behind the main building, toward the back of the business. A smaller structure, facing the side street, housed the pre-owned portion of the company. Becky threaded her way through the rows of various makes and models, keeping a wary eye out as she did so. She changed direction as a young man, obviously a salesman, looked her way. He was much too young, she decided, barely out of his teens.

Two others, neatly dressed men, were having a conversation near the building's entrance, and she rejected them as well. Finally, her eye fell on a guy of medium build who wore a shirt and tie; he stood in a relaxed manner, looking idly across the car lot. He looked older; lines bracketed his mouth, and something about the set of his shoulders caught her attention. Her instincts told her he was the person she was looking for. She let him see her peeking through the windows at the interior of one of the cars, and he approached her, a big smile lighting up his thin face.

"That's a real beauty," he said. His eyes moving over her told her he didn't necessarily mean just the car.

Becky took a deep breath, letting it raise her breasts. "I doubt I can afford this one," she murmured. She saw that the motion wasn't lost on him.

"What were you looking for, miss?"

Becky made a quarter turn away and lowered her eyes. "Something not very expensive, I'm afraid."

He took a half step closer. They were almost of the same height, she noted. "I'm sure we have something here that we can help you with," he said.

"I certainly hope so," she said so softly that he had to lean in to hear her. "I really need to find something today."

"Well, walk over this way with me," he told her. "I have a couple of things I think you might like." He stopped beside an old '60s Rambler, twenty hard years old, its paint job faded. Becky saw definite signs of rust under the door. Her lip curled with distaste before she could stop herself.

The salesman's smile wavered. "I see that this one doesn't meet your expectations, miss … what did you say your name was?" The wattage of his smile amped back up as he looked at her expectantly.

"Becky. Becky Barnes," she murmured.

"Becky Barnes," he repeated thoughtfully, moving beside her down the row of vehicles. "Why does that sound so familiar? Well, Miss Barnes, I'm Stanley Porter. Look over here. This little Pinto might be more to your liking." Suddenly, he stopped dead and snapped his fingers. "'Tarnished Rose!'" he exclaimed. "You're *that* Becky Barnes! I knew you looked familiar."

Becky felt her lips curve in her first genuine smile of the day, and she took hold of his arm, her fingers lightly clutching it as a curl of satisfaction darted through her. "That's me," she told him.

He stared at her, eyes glittering. "I can't believe it! Becky Barnes, the country singer, here on my car lot in Phillips, North Carolina!"

"Sh-h," she cautioned him, glancing around to make sure no one had heard his outburst. "I'm … kind of, um, trying to keep my being here under the radar."

"Oh, I see!" He looked around as well. "What in the world are you doing here though, Miss Barnes? You can trust me not to spread it around." He kept his voice low.

Becky leaned closer. "I'm visiting relatives," she said softly.

"Here? Here in Phillips? You have relatives here? Really?"

She nodded. "Yes," she said, making it up as she went along. "You see, something happened, uh, in my travel arrangements, and my car didn't get delivered like it was supposed to be. And I have to be somewhere this evening. That's why I'm looking to find a car. Something cheap to use just temporarily." She gave him a dazzling smile.

He stared at her, and his head bobbed up and down in a slow nod.

Becky looked at the Pinto he had indicated. Although it counted its years in double digits, it was at least ten years newer than the Rambler he'd first shown her and looked half decent; and it was red, her favorite color. "I kind of like this one," she said.

"It's a straight shift," Stanley said, looking unhappy. "Do you know how to drive a straight shift, use a clutch?"

"Oh, sure," Becky said lightly. "I learned how to drive that." She inserted her fingers into her neckline, feeling his eyes follow the action, and drew her little cache of bills out slowly, using the tips of her fingers to caress the money. His eyes followed her movement as if mesmerized. "I hope I've got enough cash here, at least for a down payment," She gazed at him intently, caressing the exposed tops of her breast over the bills under her fingertips.

Stanley cleared his throat, a flush spreading over his face. "You say there's somewhere you've got to go tonight?"

"Uh-huh."

He licked his lips. "Tell you what I'm going to do, Miss Barnes," he said. "I'm going to sign this car out to you for a test drive."

"A test drive?" she looked at him, puzzled.

"A *twenty-four-hour test drive*," he clarified, giving her a wink. "You can use it tonight without giving me any money, see if you like it, and bring it back tomorrow. You will bring it back here to me tomorrow, won't you?"

His meaning dawned on her. "Of course, I will! What do I have to do for you to give me my test drive?"

"Just sign a little piece of paper for me," Stanley said. "I just need you to fill in a local telephone number where I can reach you, along with the address where you're staying. Wait here while I go get the keys." He turned and began rapidly walking toward the office entrance.

As she watched his retreating back, it was all Becky could do not to dance.

Chapter Two

Becky had to move the car seat all the way back to accommodate her long legs. She glanced down at the fuel indicator; there was almost a full tank. She carefully pulled out across the car lot to the exit on the side street and glanced back over her shoulder. Stanley Porter stood there, watching her leave. She raised a hand in a little wave, flashed him her most blinding smile, and pulled out into the street.

On her way back to her sister's, she goosed the accelerator experimentally with minor results. The little car certainly was no sports vehicle, she reflected, but it sure beat walking. Now, if it would just hold together long enough for her to do what she needed to do.

She parked in her sister's driveway and hurried into the house. She pawed through her scattered belongings and retrieved a large, fat manila folder from the bottom of her suitcase. Briefly, she thumbed through its contents before putting it aside and riffling through the clothes piled atop the bed. She selected a body-hugging sheath dress from the mound and exchanged it for the outfit she had worn to the car lot. A pair of high-heeled pumps completed her outfit. In the bathroom, she frowned at her reflection and added more makeup, dramatizing her eyes with shadow and highlighting her cheekbones with blush.

Soon she was chugging down the highway toward a familiar destination but one she hadn't sought for more years than she cared to remember. After driving through several miles of rural country-side, she reached more urban sprawl as she made her way deeper into the adjoining county, noticing the differences from when she had last seen it. It was more developed now; businesses had disap-peared, replaced by new strip centers and unfamiliar structures. It was early afternoon, she realized, much too early for her to be where she was going.

Spotting a decent-looking restaurant up ahead, she pulled into the parking lot and went inside. Seated, she studied the menu, making careful selections that were healthy yet not pricey enough to totally deplete the few dollars she had left. She ate her meal slowly and dawdled over a cup of coffee, killing time.

When the early dinner crowd began to trickle in, she reluc-tantly paid her ticket, leaving a small tip on the table, and walked back to the Pinto.

A few miles farther on, she spotted her destination. Set a good distance back from the highway and surrounded by an enormous asphalt parking lot was a one-story, oversized block-and-corrugated metal building that loomed even larger as she turned in and drove closer. To her relief, half a dozen vehicles were pulled up close to the side of the building, including an almost-new Cadillac.

She got out and walked up to the main entrance, glancing at the posters set in the recessed glass-covered niches on either side of the door. The niches held glamour shots advertising the singers who made up the current entertainment. She pressed a button beside the door and waited. After several minutes, a small section high in the door slid back, and a pair of hostile-looking eyes glared out. "Yeah? Whatdayawant?" a deep voice growled.

Becky smiled brightly. "Jake here?" she asked.

"He's busy!" The panel started to slide shut.

"Oh, he'll want to see me," Becky said quickly. "You need to tell him that Becky Barnes is here."

"Oh, yeah?"

"Yeah!" Becky snapped. "You better tell him. He won't be very happy if he finds out I was here and you didn't let him know."

The eyes glared at her for a long moment. She stared back unflinchingly. "Wait here. I'll tell him," the man said, and the panel slid shut.

Becky stood, waiting, her manila envelope tucked under her arm. Five minutes passed as she stood watching the sun sink below the tree line off in the distance. Then ten minutes.

There was a clicking as locks disengaged. The door swung inward a foot or so, revealing a huge black man, who looked like a former linebacker, standing in the dimly lit interior. "Follow me," he growled, opening the door just wide enough for her to pass through; then it slammed shut. The locks clicked back into place, and the man began to make his way across the big room and past scores of tables, their chairs perched upside down atop them. At the far end of the room stretched a long bar, and a large, raised bandstand took up the left-hand far corner of the room.

She followed him as he made his way toward a doorway near the far right-hand corner of the room. They stepped into a dimly lit, short hallway that turned at a right angle to the left about ten feet ahead, but they halted at a closed door on the right. The man knocked once, then turned the knob and opened the door. Light spilled into the hallway; standing aside, he gestured with his chin for Becky to enter.

Becky stepped forward, her eyes adjusting to the room's brightness. She blinked, and her eyes focused on the man seated behind a large wooden desk, his back to the bare wall behind him. A pair of close-set, dark eyes gleamed under a thicket of thick, graying brows, now drawn together in a scowl. A wide, hawklike nose spilled down the center of his face above full, rosy lips, and a pair of meaty arms rested lightly before him on the desktop. The two stared at each other for a silent moment.

His lips curled upward in a smile that didn't reach his eyes. "So, it is you," he said. "To what do I owe this pleasure?"

"Hello, Jake." She advanced another step into the room, her peripheral vision taking in another muscular figure, his chair tipped backward against the wall where it made a ninety-degree angle on the left side of the room, his body looking deceptively casual and relaxed. "Long time, no see."

"I thought you was livin' the high life in Nashville," Jake said.

Becky forced a laugh. "Just visitin' my old stamping grounds," she said. "Thought I'd drop in and say hello."

His eyes made a slow survey of her, top to bottom, lingering along her body just long enough to be insulting. "You're lookin' pretty good. A little older maybe but not too bad."

"And you're just the same as always." Her voice was flat.

His eyes narrowed. "So, why are you here? What do you want from me, Becky?"

Her breath caught. "I need a gig, Jake."

"A gig?" He sounded incredulous. "You're asking to work for *me*? After you run out on me, you're crawling back, wanting a gig? What happened to that fancy-pants musician you run off with? I heard he was your manager, out there in the big time! What happened? He dump you?"

"No!" Her voice sounded high and defensive. She took a deep breath to steady herself. "I'm still with Tripp. He's … not … he's just not around right now, is all."

"Where is he?" Jake's eyes bore into her like a laser.

"He's on a road trip. He's the lead guitarist for Jackson Black's band, and right now they're on a tour around the Midwest."

Jake smiled. "An' he didn't take you along." It was a statement, not a question.

Becky gave a little half shrug. "They were keeping the head count on the tour low to keep expenses down. You know how it is. I hadn't been home in a long time, so I decided to come back for a visit while they're gone." She tried a smile. "I'm doin' you a favor, actually," she said. "Give the club a boost by having me here as a visiting headliner."

"Is that right?"

"Yeah. That's right." Their eyes clashed across the space of the room.

His lips curled derisively. "Can you still sing?"

She felt her temper flare; her fists clenched by her sides as she bit down on the response that almost slipped out of her mouth. "Yes, I can still sing," she said quietly.

He pushed back his chair and stood up. "Show me," he said. "Butch, see if Moses is around yet." He came around the desk, a short, powerfully built man with a big beer gut. The thug who had been watching their conversation brought the legs of his chair down to the floor with a thud and left the room without a word.

Jake crossed the room and took hold of Becky's arm with strong, pudgy fingers, turning her around toward the doorway. He led her back into the big, empty clubroom just as the man he had called Butch hurried through a door behind the stage, accompanied by an old, frail-looking black man. Without looking at them, the old man sat down at an upright piano on stage.

Jake gave her a little shove. "Get up there and let me hear you sing something. Butch! Turn on the mike for our visiting celeb here." He walked forward to a table near the stage, pulled a chair off it, and sat down.

Becky walked to the stage and stepped up on it, her envelope clutched under her arm. The old pianist was looking at her. He gave her a little nod of greeting as their eyes met, then looked at her expectantly. She took her place by the upright microphone at front center stage. Becky touched the mike with her fingernail, and it made an amplified thump, indicating it was on.

"Do you know 'Save the Last Dance for Me'?" she asked the old pianist. "In my key?"

The pianist raised his hands to the keyboard, and the opening notes of the song began spilling out into the silence. Becky closed her eyes and imagined herself in front of an expectant crowd; she tilted her head backward, opened her lips, and her rich voice smoothly laid out the song accompanied by the piano. As always when she sang, Becky was transported into her special place, and she *became* the song, her emotions soaring with the words.

As the last note sounded, she opened her eyes. Jake was looking up at her, his face expressionless in the dim room. He looked at the pianist and nodded curtly to the old man, who got up and scurried out. "Come 'ere," he said, beckoning to Becky.

She hopped off the low stage, walked over, and pulled another chair down from the tabletop beside him. She sank on the edge of it, looking at him expectantly.

"Okay," he said. "So, you can still sing." He pursed his lips thoughtfully. "Be here this weekend. Two shows each, Friday and Saturday nights. I'll pay you the headliner rate."

She nodded.

"Put together a list of the songs you wanna do and give it to Butch before you leave today. You gotta be here at one o'clock on Thursday, ready to rehearse with the band." He scowled at her. "Wear something sexy for the show—you know the drill. Two outfits each night. You change between the sets. You got anything we can use for publicity?"

Silently she handed him her envelope. He thumbed through

the stills. "Okay. This'll do," he said. "We can do the publicity from this."

"Uh ... Jake," she said hesitantly.

"What?"

"I, uh, need an advance."

He looked at her, his eyes flat. "Why am I not surprised?"

"I got expenses." She heard the whining note in her voice and cringed.

Without taking his eyes off her, he reached down and pulled a wad of bills from his pants pocket. Becky's eyes fixed avidly on the roll of bills as he thumbed off four hundreds and fanned them out on the tabletop. She extended her hand for them, but he snatched them back, just out of her reach.

"Uh-uh," he said. "You want an advance, you gotta earn it. You know the price of a favor from me."

Becky's breath caught in her throat. Their eyes locked; Jake's eyes glittered, and he sneered.

I'm Becky Barnes! her mind screamed silently. *You can't treat me this way*!

As the seconds ticked by, her stomach twisted, and she struggled to hold back her shiver of revulsion. *No, no*! her mind shrieked even as she knew how badly she needed this advance. She forced herself to carelessly toss her head. "No big deal," she said, relieved that her voice didn't tremble as she let him win his power struggle.

He grinned. "On your knees, girlie." There was the whine of a zipper being opened.

Becky took a deep breath. She stared at the smirk on his face as she reached out, and her fingers closed around the money. She saw the look of satisfaction in his eyes as he released the bills. She dropped to her knees on the floor between his outspread knees.

Chapter Three

It was fully dark when Becky made the turn from Pine Street into the driveway of her sister's house. She pulled up behind Clara's car and smiled to herself, remembering the look of utter relief that had lit Stanley Porter's face when she drove into the used car lot just at the end of his work shift a couple of hours ago. He had been so relieved to see her and happy, in fact, that she was able to purchase the Pinto from him for a nominal down payment of only $200.

Becky reached over and loaded her arms with the bags from the grocery store, her next stop after leaving the car lot. Approaching the side door, she saw her sister looking out at her; she brushed past Clara, who held the door open for her as she entered the kitchen and unburdened herself onto the kitchen table.

"Whose car is that you're driving?" Clara turned her pinched expression toward her.

"Mine. I bought it a little while ago."

"Where did you get the money to buy a car?"

"Same place I got the money to put some food in that bare-ass refrigerator of yours," Becky retorted. "I got me a job."

"A job? Doing what?"

Becky turned to face her. "What do you think?" she asked. "Doin' the only thing I ever did to make any real money. I'm going to be singing at Jake Reed's club this weekend. I'm going to be the headliner."

With a look of dismay, Clara stared at her sister. "Oh, Lordy," she breathed.

Becky began stowing bags of fresh vegetables into the refrigerator. "What was I supposed to do?" she asked, pausing to look over her shoulder at her sister. "I needed to make some quick money; I was broke, and for sure I didn't come here for you to support me. I'd have been outta luck if that was what I was expecting, wouldn't I? You ain't exactly living in luxury here. You've not even got anything to eat in the house."

"I usually eat up at the diner when I get off work," Clara said defensively.

"I know it, sis. I don't blame you." Becky's tone softened. "That place oughta feed you; you've been working for them forever, and considering the little bit they pay you there, they certainly oughta throw in meals."

"It's honest work," said Clara.

"I know that. So is what I do—and there's a lot more to it than just puttin' on a pretty dress and standing up there in front of a microphone and singing. And you know as well as I do that it sure pays more than what you make or what I could make if I started looking for some little job here in Phillips. If I could even find one." She gestured at her purchases. "Help yourself to any of this that you want; I had to have something to fix for me to eat if I'm going to be staying here."

"About that ... how long do you plan on staying?" ventured Clara.

"I'm not sure," Becky admitted. "I think I can manage to work at the club for three or four weeks if things go good and if I pull in a good crowd on my name recognition." Her shoulders slumped. "I don't know how long I'll be here. But I needed a job to make some money while I'm here."

Clara looked at her. "You still ain't answered the question I asked you when you first got here. What *are* you doing here, Becky? Why'd you come back to Phillips? I know for a fact that you don't have any intentions of ever coming back here permanently to live. So why are you here?"

Becky stopped putting away groceries and sat down. "Same thing I told you then. I'm not sure."

"Why now?" Clara persisted. "What brings you back now? You sure didn't have any time to come back here and help out when Mama was sick. You didn't even bother to show up for the funeral."

Becky dropped her face into her hands. "I know. I'm sorry, Clara. I'm sorry as all get-out." She looked up and saw her sister's stony expression. "You don't know how things were back then. It was like my whole world was spinning around faster and faster. Tripp was playin' six nights a week, and I was working all the time, too. I had all these gigs an' offers from this place an' that one. Three nights at this club, four at another, costume fittings, rehearsals, interviews." She felt her mind spin, remembering. "There just wasn't time for anything or anybody, and everybody was pulling at me to do this an' do that. Every minute was filled with something I had to do. It was crazy."

"And you was high as a kite with your drinking and drugs," said Clara.

"Yes! There was just so much pressure! I'd have a few drinks, sure." Becky's mouth twisted, and she stared down at the tabletop. "And somebody'd maybe lay out a few lines so we could relax, chill out. First thing I knew, I got the news from you that Mama was bad off sick. Then it seemed like only five minutes later, you called and told me that she'd died. It was too late then."

"You didn't even come home for the funeral," Clara repeated accusingly.

"I was ashamed to because I hadn't made it back here before

she died. I was under contract for a couple of gigs I couldn't get out of, and I didn't have the cash for a plane ticket back here until after I performed. And then it was too late."

There was a long silence.

"Where's Tripp at, Becky?" Clara asked at last. "Are you two still together?"

Becky looked at her. "Yeah, we're together. But it's been real hard these last couple of years. Financially, I mean. I haven't had a hit, and so it's got harder and harder for me to get gigs. We been livin' on just what Tripp made. Then he got a chance to go on tour with Jackson Black. It was a real good opportunity, so he took it. Only thing was, I couldn't go with him this time."

"Why not? You said you weren't working these days."

Becky let out a harsh sound that was supposed to be a laugh. "I haven't had a job in nearly a year," she said. "Couldn't get one."

"But … you had a hit song. It made the top fifty! You were a headliner."

"Yeah. I did. But I recorded 'Tarnished Rose' over ten years ago. Can you believe it? Ten years!" Becky shook her head. "They called me a rising star. I made a demo, and I was playing on the radio two months after I got there. Then when I recorded 'Tarnished Rose' and it went into the top one hundred nationally … oh, my God! We were on cloud nine! The money just poured in, and we lived it up! The next one was really gonna make me a star. But nothing else I did caught on after that. Once you get a big one, if you don't keep on producing hits, one right after another, you're forgotten. That's it for you. You're worse than a has-been—you're a nobody."

"So, is that why you've come back home then? Because you can't get a job?"

Becky shook her head furiously. "No! I'm not finished. There'll be another hit—I just have to find the right song."

"Then why? Why have you come back, after all this time?

I know you didn't come back to Phillips to see me." Her voice dripped with sarcasm.

Becky slowly shook her head.

"Why, Becky?" Clara's voice softened. "What's going on?"

Becky was silent, staring off into space. Finally, her lips moved, almost in a whisper. "I wanted to see Benjie," she said.

Clara's whole body stiffened; her mouth dropped open. "Benjie? You came back to Phillips to see Benjie?"

Becky bit her lip and bowed her head.

Clara shook her head emphatically. "Forget it! That's just not possible!" she snapped, then continued in a milder tone. "Why, after all this time, do you want to stir things up?"

"I don't know," Becky confessed. "I just know that I need to see him."

Clara got to her feet and took hold of one of Becky's bags of food, busying herself by helping to put the items away. "You know Quinn will never let you anywhere near him."

Becky shrugged.

"Did you know he's married again?" Clara muttered. She stopped and stared at her sister. "He's remarried, and him and his wife have got a little boy an' a little girl of their own, along with Benjie. You'd be best off to leave them alone! What do you mean comin' back here to cause trouble, after all these years? What's it been, fifteen years now?"

"Fourteen," Becky corrected her in a low voice. "Benjie'd be fourteen years old now."

"Exactly! So what possible good would it do for you to just show up, out of the blue, an' cause trouble?"

"I don't mean to cause trouble. I just want to see him. That's all."

"Oh, right!" Clara threw up her hands. "And just what do you plan to say to that boy? 'Hey, Benjie, I'm your long-lost mama! I left your daddy when you was just three months old. I ran off with another man, just abandoned you an' your daddy. Now come here an' give me a big ol' hug an' a kiss to welcome me back into your life'? Do you honestly think that Quinn will let you see him?"

"I don't know," Becky said miserably.

"Well, just forget it! You'd best pack up your bag an' head back to Nashville!"

"I want to see him," Becky said.

"Why?" Clara's raised voice echoed in the room.

"I don't know! I just want to see how he turned out."

Clara let out an exasperated sigh.

"How is Quinn, anyway?" Becky asked in a small voice.

"Oh, Quinn's just fine! He built up that business of his—the one he was just starting when you run out on him—and he's doin' great. All of them—Quinn, Donna, and their little ones—they go to church every Sunday over at the Methodist church. He's a respected member of the community."

"Quinn?" A small smile curved Becky's lips.

"Yeah, Quinn! An' his new wife's a teacher over at the elementary school. They're good folks, an' they're happy. Don't you come back here and cause trouble, Becky! You hear me?"

"I have no intention of causing anybody any trouble," she replied. "I just feel like I need to see my little boy. That's all."

"And what happens then?" asked Clara. She sat down at the table, all the bags of groceries put away. "After you see Benjie, I mean. Are you going to get him all excited about finding his 'real' mother and then take off and leave him again? I know you're not plannin' to stay here. What happens after you go back to Nashville? You do plan to go back to Nashville and back to Tripp, don't you?"

"Well, sure, I'll go back. Tripp will be back home from the tour soon."

"So, what about Benjie? You can't take him back with you. When will you come back here again? How often do you plan on seeing him?"

"I don't know," said Becky. "I hadn't thought about that yet."

"Well, you'd better think about it," Clara said grimly. "You need to think about Benjie."

"I'm going to! But I've got to be able to talk to him first."

"Look, Becky," Clara said. "You've got to realize that you just can't have everything you want. You left Quinn and Benjie because you ran off with Tripp. Do you still want to be with Tripp?"

"Of course, I do! I love Tripp."

"How's he feel about your coming here?"

"He doesn't know," Becky said softly.

"He doesn't know!" repeated Clara incredulously. "My God, Becky! What are you telling me?"

"Well, he was gone. He left me by myself in Nashville when he took the job traveling with the tour group." Becky's voice rose defensively. She bit her lip.

Clara just looked at her without comment.

"I … I got to thinking about Benjie. I wondered how he looked, what he was doing …" Becky's voice trailed off.

"What do you think Tripp is going to say when he finds out you're here?" asked Clara.

"I don't know." Becky raised her head and looked at Clara. "I just know that I really needed to come here. He'll just have to understand."

"Do you think he will?"

"Yeah. He'll have to."

"Look," Clara insisted. "You've got to think this thing through, Becky. After Benjie finds out who you are, how long are you going to stay here? Do you plan to be part of his life?"

"Yes," said Becky. "I want to."

"How are you going to do that?" asked Clara.

"I don't know yet," said Becky. "But I do know that I'm going to work it out. I have to."

Chapter Four

A week passed. Becky found life in Phillips pretty empty. The days crawled by, and she spent time alone, since Clara was at work, and she no longer knew anyone to spend time with or talk to. The following Wednesday, she got up late in the morning—long after the time Clara had risen and departed for her early-morning shift at the diner. She ate some fruit and yogurt, and drank two mugs of coffee in the silent house.

Trying to decide how to fill the empty hours of her day, she wandered out into the front yard, meandering aimlessly around, random memories from her childhood running through her head. She halted, feeling a strange sensation on the back of her neck. Slowly turning, she saw a woman standing in the yard of the house next door, staring at her. Racking her brain to try to place her, Becky turned and made her way toward that side of the yard.

"Hello, there." She put on her best meet-the-public smile. "How you doing?"

The woman took several reluctant-looking steps toward her. She was dressed in a shapeless housedress under a sagging unbuttoned cardigan sweater, her head tipped to one side as she stared frankly at Becky, frowning. "Hey," she said. "Do I know you?"

Becky stopped just at the edge of Clara's yard. "I'm not sure," she said, her smile still brightly in place. "I'm Becky. I'm Clara's sister."

The woman nodded. "Thought that was who you were," she acknowledged. "I'm Patsy Pardue." She squinted up at Becky. "You here for a visit with Clara?"

"That's right," Becky acknowledged. She held out her hand, and the woman reluctantly advanced and briefly let her fingers be taken by Becky's.

"Clara at work?"

"Yes. She is."

The woman's eyes glittered. "Don't you live off away from here somewhere?"

"That's right," said Becky. "I live in Nashville."

"That's what I thought. How long you here for?"

Becky was growing more and more uncomfortable under the woman's unrelenting gaze. "Oh, I'm here just for a short visit," she said airily, taking a step backward.

"Yeah. I been seeing a strange car in Clara's driveway. That yours? But it's got North Carolina plates on it. I thought you lived in another state."

"That's my car," acknowledged Becky. "I just got it to use while I'm here," she told her, backing away. "It was nice to see you, Ms. Pardue."

"Nice to meetcha." The woman continued to stare at her as Becky made a retreat back into the house.

"Wow," Becky said to herself as she let the side door close behind her. "I forgot how nosy everybody around here is." Wandering back through the house, she decided she would drive around town and refamiliarize herself with the place she had left behind. Maybe she'd drive down to the center of town, park, and walk around. See what all had changed. Probably very little, she mused.

Late that afternoon, Becky strolled past the front entrance of Phillips Elementary School. She'd been drawn back here but not by her memories, although this was where she and Clara had gone to school in what seemed like a lifetime ago. Today she kept thinking about Benjie—this was the place where he was growing up. He would likely eat an ice cream cone at the drugstore, maybe ride a bike on these streets. But the place she knew for sure where he would be was here—the school. It drew her back yet again.

She hung around for at least an hour; the last of the big, yellow buses pulled out, and only a scattering of cars remained parked in the lot just to the side of the school. She approached the wide steps leading up to the double-door front entrance of the old brick building just as one of the pair of doors swung outward and a small, slender woman came hurrying out. The woman paused for half a step when she saw Becky; then she altered her course slightly to approach her.

"Hello," she said, big brown eyes looking up at Becky, a friendly smile on her face. "Can I help you? Are you waiting for someone? One of our students?"

"No," Becky told her. "I, uh, I used to live here. As a matter of fact, I went to school here, and I was just looking around. Remembering things." She gave a short laugh and ducked her head.

"It probably hasn't changed too much." The woman's smile widened. "Although, as you probably will recall, this campus used to house all twelve grades before the county consolidated all the high schools into two new ones a few years ago. Now there's an East High School not too far from here and a West High over on the other side of the county. This is just the elementary school. But we've added a kindergarten now, so it's got grades k through eight here." She cocked her head to one side, looking up at Becky. "I'm Mrs. Cavanaugh," she added. "I teach first grade here."

Becky's heart lurched. *Mrs. Cavanaugh. Quinn's wife. Of all the people to run into,* she thought. "I'm Becky Barnes," she said automatically.

Donna Cavanaugh gave a small nod and continued to smile at her with no sign of recognition. The name Becky Barnes obviously meant nothing to her. Becky permitted herself to breathe again.

There was the sound of hurrying footsteps behind her. Becky glanced around just as a young adolescent, towing another, younger boy by the hand, started up the steps toward them.

"Well, about time you got here." The warm tone of Donna Cavanaugh's voice belied her words. She bent down to the younger boy's level as he came to a halt in front of her. "Did you have a nice day today, Sammy? What did you do today?"

"They were finger painting when I went to get him," the older boy said. "That's what made me late—he had to wash up."

Becky stared at him, unable to catch her breath. He was slim and athletic looking, but there was already a promise of width in the boy's shoulders; he had light-brown hair and a sprinkle of freckles across his nose, but the hazel eyes that glanced over at her curiously were carbon copies of hers!

Her mouth went dry, and she froze.

"These are my sons, Benjie and Sammy," Donna said. "Say hello to Ms. Barnes." She straightened up and turned her attention back to Becky.

"Hello, Ms. Barnes," Benjie said.

"H'llo," echoed the smaller boy.

Becky nodded, unable to tear her gaze from Benjie.

"Well, nice seeing you," Donna told her. "I hope you enjoy your stay here in Phillips. Come on, boys, let's go pick up your sister from Grandma's and get on home."

Becky stood, watching them walk away from her toward the parking lot. "Benjie," she whispered, her eyes filling and a wave of yearning washing over her. She wanted to scream, to run after them, to grab the boy and crush him to her. It took everything she had to simply stand there and watch them walk away.

Chapter Five

Becky had a hard time concentrating during her Thursday rehearsal at Jake's; she could think of nothing except the problem of how she might find a way to talk with her son. Over and over, she thought of ways to approach him, discarding each in turn.

The band consisted of a drummer, two guitarists, and the old man, Moses, who played the piano. Moses was the only one of them who had been there when Becky worked for Jake all those years ago. After she flubbed the lyrics to a standard country song twice, Moses held up his hand to pause the session, stood up, and walked over to her.

"Look, missy," he said quietly to her, "I don't mean no disrespect, but it might be best if you put whatever it is you got on your mind aside. Mr. Jake, he's gonna be in here shortly, an' he ain't gonna be none too happy with what's happening here today." He shook his head. "If you don't sound good, real smooth and professional, it won't be pretty. He'll have you outta here in a heartbeat. Don't matter to him if you're a famous singer somewhere else."

Becky looked at the old man, seeing the honest concern written on his face. She nodded. "You're right," she said. "Let's do this one over."

Moses walked back over to his piano. "Let's take it again, boys," he said. "From the top."

When Jake and his two goons walked in later that afternoon, he paused on his way back to his office. Becky was belting out a rendition of a Tammy Wynette hit. He listened for a moment, then nodded and walked on. The remainder of their rehearsal had gone well; they had run through the entire selection of songs Becky had chosen for Friday night's performance three times. When they finished her final song this time, she walked over to Moses, who was seated on his piano bench.

"Thank you," she said, giving him a significant look. She saw that he understood what she meant.

He gave a slight nod. "You're welcome, Miss Barnes," he said formally. "You comfortable with everything now? Anything you want us to run through for you again?"

"No, I think we're good," she said.

He nodded. "I like that you're opening the second set with your big hit."

Becky smiled. He knew that was her big hit; she hadn't mentioned it. "Yeah. I usually do that. The crowd expects to hear it sooner or later during the evening, and that's a surefire way to get their attention back—especially when I haven't sung it during the first set."

"Okay. See you tomorrow night then."

Becky got to the club early on Friday—about six o'clock. She wanted to make sure everything was perfect for her premier appearance.

She looked critically at the newly installed posters of her on either side of the front door as she crept past in her little Pinto. Her head-shots didn't look bad, she thought. "Special limited appearance—Nashville's own Becky Barnes" screamed the big red letters at the top of the poster. She nodded. It would do.

She eased into a parking spot near the side door. Half a dozen cars were already here. She got out and, reaching into the back seat, pulled out her two costume changes on their hangers and carefully locked the car. She felt the first little hitch of excitement as she pulled open the side door and nodded to Jake's man, who was leaning against the wall and keeping tabs on the entrance. He gave her the barest of nods in return as she walked toward one of the two tiny closets back of the stage that served as dressing rooms.

As she neared the one assigned to her, the door to the adjoining room flew open. A pretty, young woman glared at her, backlit from the room behind her. Her blonde hair flowed in riotous waves down her back, and her round blue eyes spat fire as she raked her eyes over Becky.

"So, you're the great Becky Barnes," she said.

Becky halted and looked coolly at her, her costumes casually slung over her shoulder. "Yeah. Who's askin'?"

"'Who's askin'?'" the blonde mimicked. "I'm the one you stole the headliner spot from. That's who!" Her blue eyes narrowed. "I was up for it, and you waltzed in and stole it from me!" Her voice rose shrilly. "I'm the one whose picture was supposed to be out there tonight!"

"Whoa, whoa," said Becky. "I don't know what you're talking about. I don't even know who you are!"

The blonde raised her hands, fingers splayed into claws. "How many BJs did you have to give Jake to take my spot away from me?" she shrilled. "Everybody here knows how that works!" She obviously hadn't seen the shadowy figure move silently up behind her until Jake's man, Butch, laid a hand on her shoulder and gripped it hard. She jerked her head around. Butch looked down at her, his eyes cold.

"Hadn't you better get dressed, Susanna?" he said in a low voice. "Jake won't like it if you ain't ready for your opening number."

She tried to shrug off the big hand that gripped her shoulder, but Butch maintained his hold on her, and they locked eyes. Susanna broke the stare first. She lowered her head meekly and bit her lip. "Okay, Butch," she said. He released her, and she went back into the dressing room, rubbing her shoulder. The hallway lighting dimmed as her door closed behind her. Butch looked at Becky.

"You're early," he said.

Becky nodded. She stepped past him as he moved back half a step to let her pass. She moved into her dressing room and switched on the light; she felt her heart pounding, and her feeling of happy anticipation was gone. She hung her dresses on the metal pole serving as a closet rod and slipped out of her jacket. She heard voices outside, that of a woman and the heavier grumble of a male. Becky stripped down to her underwear. Switching on the lights that bordered a mirror hung over the low chest, which served as a makeup table, she sat down on her stool and began smoothing on the heavy foundation she used for the stage. Someone rapped on her door.

"Come in." She twisted around to face the door as it opened a few inches, and Butch poked his head in.

"Everything's good," he said, his face impassive, ignoring her unclothed state. "She won't cause you no more trouble." The door closed.

"Thanks!" Becky called out to the closed door. He was gone. *What the hell?* she wondered as she turned back to her mirror and went back to applying her stage makeup. She shrugged.

There was always drama here; that was one thing that never failed. As long as she could remember, Jake's place had had a reputation for being on the shady side, and most folks looked down on it. But it was the only place anywhere around that offered a venue where you could hear live entertainment, and it drew a good crowd because of that. Then there was the fact that there was never any real trouble here. Drama, yes, but Jake and his crew kept a tight rein on things. They were known for that.

She went back to applying her stage makeup. Shortly after that, she heard the faint sound of the band tuning up coming through the flimsy walls. She hummed a few bars of her opening number as she reached for the green satin dress she had brought to use for her first set. If she listened hard, she could hear the opening singer and the sporadic clapping that followed.

Please let there be a good crowd tonight, she prayed as she dug into her tote bag for a bottle of water. Drinking deeply, she sat down on the single armless chair that sat over by the back wall of the small room and closed her eyes. Trying to relax, she rested her head against the wall.

She must have succeeded because she started and her heart leaped when sometime later someone rapped on her door. A male voice outside announced loudly, "Ten minutes!"

Becky slipped the dress off its hanger and quickly zipped it up her back. Slipping into her five-inch heels, she threw a backward look at the mirror. Her reflection showed a tall, broad-shouldered woman with cascading auburn hair and a deeply rouged, wide mouth, her eyes expertly dramatized. She smoothed the form-fitting fabric down her hips and walked out of her dressing room and toward the spot at the back of the stage, from which she would step up and make her entrance. The lead guitarist was announcing her. "Now, straight from Nashville, ladies and gentlemen, here's the hit country star—Miss Becky Barnes!"

She plastered a huge smile on her face and stepped out to a round of applause from the nearly filled room. Expectant faces turned up toward her as she walked out behind the standing mike into the spotlight, and the band began to play the opening of her first number. Becky felt alive in every cell of her body.

Chapter Six

On Sunday, Becky woke in a sun-filled room. She got out of bed groggily, squinted in the cheerful light, and padded into the kitchen, where she started a pot of coffee. After she poured a cup and inhaled the rich aroma rising from it, she slid a slice of bread into the toaster and sat down, sipping the hot liquid. Only then did she take a look at the kitchen clock.

Jesus, it was going on one o'clock! She'd slept almost eight hours since letting herself into the still, dark house the night before.

When the toaster popped, she retrieved the piece of dry bread and poured herself a refill of coffee. Hearing a noise behind her, she turned to see her sister entering the side door and wearing a brown, two-piece suit instead of her usual waitress uniform.

"You finally decide to get up?" Clara commented, closing the door behind her.

"Yeah. I was *working* last night, remember?" Becky shot back. "You been to church, I presume."

Clara nodded, got down a mug, and helped herself to some coffee. "How did your evening go?" she asked.

Becky raised an eyebrow, surprised by her interest. "Good. Pretty good. Jake said business was a little bit up from usual. He actually said he expected next weekend to be even better, when the word gets around that I'm appearing. I guess I'm still considered famous around here."

"Well, that's good, I guess," said Clara.

Becky stood up and snagged her purse from where she'd dropped it on the hall table when she came in the night before. She opened it and pulled out two one-hundred-dollar bills. She tossed one of them on top of the table in front of Clara.

"What's that for?" asked her sister.

"Jake paid me the rest of what he owed me for the weekend. He's a real jerk, but at least he's honest when it comes to paying his help what they're due. Take that. I made a couple of long-distance calls on your phone."

Clara eyed the money. "I'm sure you didn't talk a hundred dollars' worth."

"Look, just take it, okay? You're giving me a place to stay. It's the least I can do."

Clara picked up the money and looked at it, caressing it between her fingers. "Do you know how long I'd have to work for that at my job?" she asked.

"Yeah. I know. You work your ass off and don't make squat." Becky's expression softened. "I also know I owe you a whole lot more than that. Okay?"

They both sipped coffee. Clara broke the silence. "Have you decided what you're going to do?"

Becky shook her head slowly. She let out a long sigh. "I don't know how I'm going to get to talk to Benjie. I've run out of ideas. I guess the only thing I can do is to go talk to Quinn and ask for his permission."

"Are you sure that's a good idea?"

"No," Becky said. "It's an awful idea." She spread out her hands. "But what else can I do?"

"Quinn's a hard man," Clara said musingly. "I doubt very seriously that he's going to let you anywhere near Benjie."

"I have to try."

Clara looked across the room unseeingly. "He never had anything much to do with any of us after you left," she said. "Mama tried, before she got so bad sick, to get Quinn to bring Benjie over here every once in a while, so he'd know we were family, too. But between Quinn and that mother of his ..."

"You don't have to tell me anything about Quinn's mother! We lived with her after we got married and before I had Benjie, remember? You can't tell me nothing new about that ol' witch!" Becky looked at Clara. "Are you telling me that they wouldn't let Mama see her own grandson?"

Clara shrugged. "Yeah, once in a great while, we'd get to see him. But most times when Mama wanted to see him, seemed like they always was too busy or had something else to do. We didn't get to see him very often. And now that Quinn's remarried an' him an' Donna have got kids of their own as well as Benjie—well, even before that, after Mama died, it got so that I didn't hardly ever see him at all. I don't know if he even knows I'm his aunt."

"I ran into his new wife the other day," confided Becky.

"Oh, yeah? Donna's a real nice lady," Clara said quickly. "What did she have to say?"

"She didn't know who I was." Becky let out a short laugh.

"Well, if you ask me, you oughta keep it like that. In my opinion, it's not a very good idea telling Quinn you want to see Benjie."

"What else can I do?" Becky asked.

Clara shook her head.

Early on Monday morning, Becky got into her little Pinto and drove over to her ex-husband's business. Approaching it, she saw that the site was a beehive of activity, and it was much larger than she had imagined it would be. Two or three dump trucks and a big flatbed trailer that was hauling a backhoe pulled out onto the highway from the property while she sat, signaling to make the left turn across the road into the wide entrance in front of the long metal building serving as the office area. Behind the building, a chain-link fence enclosed a huge parking area with a dozen or more pieces of heavy-duty equipment parked on the neat, gravel lot. She saw half a dozen men walking around the area, busily working.

Quinn had done well, she realized, impressed. He'd come a very long way. She fought down her rising trepidation as she got out of her car.

She climbed the concrete-form steps in front of the door and pulled it open. Just inside, a man looked up from behind a battered desk. "Can I help you, ma'am?" he asked politely as she hesitated in the doorway.

"I'm looking for Quinn Cavanaugh," Becky told him.

At the sound of her voice, a tall, broad-shouldered man rose from a swivel chair behind a second desk to the left and stared at her. "Becky?" he said incredulously.

"Hello, Quinn," she replied.

He took two strides in her direction. "What are you doing here, Becky?" His voice was low and calm, but those wintry blue eyes she remembered so well stared at her forbiddingly.

"I need to talk to you, Quinn," she replied, her breath catching in her throat. She'd forgotten just how big and male he was, what an aura of power and intimidation surrounded him; it had turned her on like an aphrodisiac back in the days when they were together. Now she raised her chin, determined not to let it back her down in the slightest. "It's about Benjie."

There was a flash of alarm in his frosty eyes before his face showed no expression at all. He raised one eyebrow. "What about

Benjie?" He glanced over at the man behind the other desk, who was avidly listening to every word. "Take a break, Brett," he said in a steely voice. The man rose to his feet without a word and hurried out of the office, the door banging shut behind him.

Quinn's eyes impaled her as the door closed. "I said, 'What about Benjie?'" he repeated.

"I want to see him." Becky stood her ground.

"Not a chance!"

"Come on, Quinn!" Becky softened her voice. "I just want to see my boy, talk to him. After all, I *am* his mother."

"Like hell you are!" Quinn's voice thundered. "What are you trying to do, Becky, after all these years? Do you think you can just waltz in here, right out of the blue, and disrupt Benjie's life?" His eyes narrowed. "What are you really up to?"

"Nothing! I just want to see him!"

"Do you expect me to believe that?"

"Believe what you want to. It's the truth," cried Becky.

"You wouldn't know the truth if it bit you on the ass!"

They glared at each other. Becky took a deep breath. "Look, Quinn, let's start over," she cajoled. "Is it asking too much for me to want to see my son?"

"Yeah. It is! Especially since you just up and left him when he was a helpless little baby, and you haven't shown one minute of interest in him since then. Where were you all those years when I was the one looking after him? Huh? Where were you then?"

"I know I've made a lot of mistakes."

"Mistakes! You call it making mistakes when you just up and abandon your own child?"

"I'm sorry." Tears spilled out of her eyes.

"Sorry! Sorry doesn't cut it, Becky!" He slammed his hand down hard on the desktop. "Now you better get your butt outta here, right now." He looked thunderously at her. "And you'd better not come anywhere near Benjie. Do you hear me? You stay away from him. And if you know what's good for you, you'll get out of here and go right back to Nashville or wherever it is that you're living now."

Becky backed away from his fury. "You haven't heard the last from me, Quinn," she said softly.

"It had better be the last. Just get out of here. And you stay away from Benjie. You stay away from my boy."

Becky slipped through the door, hurried down the steps, got in her car, and drove quickly away.

Her hands were shaking so badly that she could barely keep the Pinto in its lane as she drove the short distance back into town; instinctively she headed down Main Street, U-turned, and parked crookedly in a spot on the street that an old Buick had just pulled out of. Half running, she stumbled into the diner.

Heads lifted from their plates of bacon, eggs, and pancakes as she pushed the door open and rushed in. Clara stopped dead still behind the counter. Slowly she set the coffee carafe back on the burner and hurried out to meet her sister in the middle of the room. With her face full of concern, she put her hand on Becky's arm and with a gentle tug urged her toward an empty back booth.

"I guess I don't have to ask you how it went," she said softly, half pushing Becky into the booth. She glanced around the room. The diners were resuming their eating, pretending that their real focus was not on the little drama taking place behind them.

"Oh, Clara, you were right! I shouldn't have gone there. I just made things a thousand times worse," Becky burst out, her face anguished.

"Sh-h," Clara cautioned her. "You sit right here. I'll get you a cup of coffee. It's about time for my break anyway. I'm going to sit down here with you, and you can tell me what happened."

As Clara scurried away, Becky looked around. The diner was about half empty; it was late enough for most of the breakfast crowd to have left already. She saw two or three people sneaking openly curious looks at her; they quickly dropped their eyes when they saw her looking back at them. Becky took a deep, shuddering breath and looked down at her trembling hands as Clara returned, bringing two of the heavy, white mugs filled with steaming coffee. She slid into the booth across from Becky, her face creased with concern.

"Tell me," she said simply.

Becky grasped the proffered hot mug with both hands. "You were right," she said. "I should never have gone over there."

"Okay. What did he say?"

Becky's face twisted with misery. She took a deep breath, letting it out slowly. "He yelled at me. Told me to get out and go back to Nashville, where I belong."

Clara sighed. "Did you expect him to welcome you with open arms?"

"Well, no. Of course not." Becky angrily dashed away an errant tear trickling down her cheek. "But I just made things worse."

Clara sighed. She picked up her mug and looked across the top of it at Becky. "So, what are you going to do now?" She set her coffee back down.

"I don't know!"

Neither of them drank any coffee.

"Quinn's got a lot of influence here now," Clara spoke softly, almost to herself. "If he's decided that you can't see Benjie, he'll be able to keep you from him. Legally, I mean."

Becky leaned her forehead against her fisted hand and made a whimpering sound.

Clara set her untouched coffee down on the tabletop. She took a deep breath. "I have an idea."

"What?"

"Let me go make a phone call. You sit right here; I'll be back in a minute." Becky watched Clara slide out, walk purposefully across the room, back behind the counter, and pick up the telephone. Clara spoke briefly into the phone, then stood there, holding the receiver to her ear for several minutes before conducting a brief conversation and replacing the receiver. There was a satisfied glint in her eyes when she slid back into the booth.

"Who did you call?" Becky asked suspiciously.

"Donna, Quinn's wife."

Becky opened her lips to speak, but Clara overrode her, speaking quickly and softly. "You go on home now. But come back here to the diner at three o'clock sharp. I asked Donna to come here just as soon as the last bell rings. I told her that I needed to talk to her, that it was real important."

"And she agreed to come?" Becky frowned skeptically.

Clara shrugged. "Yeah, she did. That's all I told her—just that it was real important." She leaned forward. "Now, you better be here at three o'clock!"

"Oh, I will."

"Go on home now." Clara gathered up the still-full mugs and started to get up. "You just make sure you're here. Don't you make a fool out of me, Becky!"

Becky got to her feet. "Thank you, Clara," she said, but her sister was already halfway back to the counter and didn't appear to hear her.

Chapter Seven

Half an hour later, Becky walked into the kitchen and dropped her tote bag on one of the high-back chairs. She wanted a drink worse than she had in recent memory. She began opening cabinets, knowing her sister didn't keep liquor in the house, but she was so full of nervous energy and need that she looked anyway. Finally, she dropped down on one of the chairs and put her hands over her face. *God in heaven, I need a drink!*

Slowly, her head sank down to her folded arms, and her swirling thoughts took her back to the first time she ever saw Quinn Cavanaugh.

Against the wishes of her family and partly in defiance of their objections, she had been working on Friday and Saturday nights at Jake's roadhouse for about six months back then. She had been one of the two girls who sang as the opening and closing acts for the headliner. She had always been told what a wonderful singing voice she had been blessed with, but Phillips, North Carolina, sure didn't offer any opportunities to use it, unless you counted singing in the church choir on Sundays.

Her mother almost had a cow when she, along with two of her giggling classmates, drove down to Jake's, and she was the one who came back home with a new job. After her screaming arguments, pouting, and threats to quit school in the middle of her senior year in high school, her mother finally and grudgingly agreed that she could try the job, thinking that the novelty would soon wear off and that Becky would quit. But that hadn't happened, and the longer Becky worked, the more she craved the rush she got when the applause flowed around her after she sang, and the bigger her dreams of stardom grew. Jake's was just a steppingstone, she figured, just the first step on her way to big things and big money. She blissfully brushed away the wandering hands, ignored the liquor-smelling breath of Jake's customers, and kept working.

Of course, her reputation at school hadn't been helped when word got around of where she was working. Always somewhat of a wild child, though accepted, she had never been part of the popular crowd. Having those prim and proper girls nudge each other and whisper behind their hands as she walked by was nothing new. She even relished her new popularity among certain of her male classmates and picked and chose, dating those who appealed to her and stingily allocating her sexual favors only if they suited her in the moment.

Becky wasn't a virgin; that bridge had been crossed back when she was only fourteen, the big act done solely to satisfy her curiosity as to what the fuss was all about and done with a pimply faced cousin, whom she promptly forgot all about. She was selective, she told herself. Going out with her didn't mean sex was a sure thing, but that hint of possibility, along with her pickiness, only added to her appeal among her male classmates. At school, Becky was having the time of her life.

Jake liked his two openers to mingle with his customers between their sets. Their presence while wandering through the room and chatting with the customers encouraged bigger bar tabs; conversation was all he required of them, but smiling conversation with the customers was an unspoken obligation.

Therefore, one Saturday night Becky was leaning up against

the bar, chatting up the bartender in the early evening before her first set, when her eye caught the entrance of three burly males. She particularly noticed the one in the middle, who walked across the room toward the bar with a graceful, catlike stride like he owned the place.

He was tall and broad shouldered, his body lithe and muscular, with his arms swinging loosely at his sides. All three wore tight, faded jeans; scuffed, low-heeled boots; and leather jackets, even though it was a warm June night.

Bikers, Becky thought.

They took stools near her, and the bartender eased away from her to serve them.

She watched from under lowered lashes as they talked and laughed easily, clearly enjoying a relaxed friendship. A second round of beers was soon ordered; one of them slid off his stool and wandered over toward the jukebox, leaving the place next to the tall one open. Becky moved casually beside him and started to slide her butt up onto the empty stool. "Is this place taken?" she murmured as he glanced quickly at her.

He turned toward her. "It is now," he said, raising his beer to his lips and staring frankly at her over the bottle. He had the palest blue eyes Becky had ever seen, contrasting sharply with his dark-brown hair and tanned face. Suddenly, a shock of recognition ran through her. She knew this guy.

"Can I buy you a beer, pretty lady?" he said. His eyes narrowed. "Or are you even old enough to drink?"

"I'm old enough," Becky retorted, stung. "But I prefer a Coke. I'm singing later." She raised her chin.

"Singing?" His drawl conveyed amusement and disbelief.

"Yes! I do one of the opening sets," she told him proudly.

"Well! I can't wait to hear it." He turned to his companion. "Hear that, Jim? She says she's part of the entertainment."

The man leaned forward, looking her over with a leering grin. "I don't doubt it a bit," he said. "She can entertain me anytime."

The bartender set a highball glass filled with Coca-Cola and ice in front of her. He lifted a brow at the men.

"Yeah, I'll have another," said the tall man's companion. "Another round here."

Becky picked up her soda and sipped it. She threw another flirtatious look toward him.

"My name's Quinn." He accepted his new beer and raised it, his pale eyes intense. "What do I call you, pretty lady?"

"Becky." Her heart pounded as she surveyed him covertly, searching her mind for what she knew about him. Quinn Cavanaugh, she remembered, was just back home in Phillips from a stint in the Marine Corps. He was four or five years older than she, with his whispered-about bad-boy reputation from his high school days. He'd roar through town on his motorcycle with that I-don't-give-a-damn-what-you-think-about-me attitude of his. She suppressed a shiver as she looked at him—tall enough that she could look up at him! —and felt that sheer power of sex appeal just radiating off him.

"Hey, Becky!" The bartender broke the spell. "Shouldn't you be going backstage? It's almost time for you to go on."

"Yeah, thanks, Bill," she said, sliding off the stool. She turned to Quinn. "Will you be here when I finish?"

His lips turned up in a small smile. "Sure. I'll hang around."

She flashed him a smile and hurried away.

Becky stepped up to the mike as the smattering of applause died down after her introduction. She glanced across to the bar. True to his word, he was still sitting there. She gave her signal, and the band launched into her first song.

That night, Becky put every ounce of her energy into her per-formance. As her third and last song finished and she made her little bow, she was rewarded by a burst of longer-than-usual applause from her audience, and even one or two catcalls rang out.

Gratified and flushed, she hurried off the stage to the rear as the other girl singer was being announced. She made her way back toward the bar. The stool next to Quinn was now occupied, so she insinuated her body next to him; he was watching the new singer, his face expressionless.

"Well? What did you think?" she said, her voice sounding breathless next to his ear.

His head turned, and he gave her a lazy smile. "Very nice. I enjoyed it, Becky."

She willed herself not to wriggle with pleasure. He slid off his stool and stood. "Where are you going?" she asked, a note of dismay in her voice.

"I got to go. It's been a long week."

Becky took hold of his arm. "Where are your friends?" she asked.

"Over there." He pointed with his chin. She followed his gaze to see them sitting with a pair of women at a nearby table. Judging from where his hands were positioned on the woman's body, one of them had already gotten to second base and was headed to third. The four of them had their heads turned toward the stage, appearing to be listening to the singer, while hands were roaming. Quinn chuckled. "Don't think they'll miss me."

"I'm here every weekend—every Friday and Saturday night," Becky said quickly. "Will you come back again?"

He looked down at her upturned face. "Maybe." He moved then, placed his hands one on either side of her waist, fingers spread, and held her lightly. "You're a tasty-looking little morsel. You know that?" A little smile lit his eyes. "Maybe I will be seeing you soon." He let go of her and turned away, striding toward the exit. Her eyes followed him until he disappeared out the door.

Becky rubbed her face, remembering how disappointed she had been when the next weekend passed without Quinn showing up at the club. But he had come in the following weekend on Saturday night. She was onstage, looking out across the room at the blur of faces turned toward her, listening, when suddenly she spotted him, walking toward the bar.

Her heart gave an unexpected lurch, and she almost faltered on the lyrics. Recovering quickly, she finished the number and smiled brightly as applause broke out. The band segued into her final song, and she felt her energy bubble up as she belted out her lament to heartbreak and lost love.

He raised his beer bottle in salute as she approached him at the bar. "So, you decided to come back?" she said, and even she heard how lame her comment sounded.

"I did." He gave a hard look at the man sitting next to him. The man picked up his drink and slid off the stool, making a hasty retreat. "Here, I saved you a seat." Quinn grinned.

Becky laughed and sat down.

She never remembered what they talked about that night, but she remembered clearly what happened after she sang her closing set. The club was full that night, and Quinn took her arm and guided her toward the exit after she left the stage for her second and final time that evening and approached him at the bar.

Once they were out the door, he steered her to the relatively dark area at the front corner of the building. Pushing her up against the cool siding, he captured her in his muscular arms and gave her the most thorough kiss of her life. When he raised his head, her knees were wobbly, and she clung to him for balance.

"How did you get here?" His voice was hoarse.

"I ... I drove. My car's parked near the back."

"Where do you live?"

"Same place you do," she told him. "I live in Phillips."

She had the satisfaction of seeing the look of sheer surprise on his face. "Son of a gun!" he exclaimed. "Why don't I know you?"

She almost laughed. "Darned if I know."

"I'll follow you home," he growled. "Is there anything back in there you need to get?"

"My purse."

"Get it then!"

Becky gave him one last searching look before going back into the club. He was already astride his bike, the big Harley growling with muted power, when she reappeared. She gave him a little wave and climbed into her mother's old car. He eased the bike up beside the driver's side door, and she rolled down her window when he made a circling motion with his hand.

"You know that little picnic area by the creek at the last exit before you get to Phillips?" he asked. "Pull off there," he told her when she nodded. He roared off before she could say a word. Becky put the car into drive and followed him down the highway.

He was leaning up against his bike, his helmet was off and resting on the bike seat, when she pulled off the highway onto the gravel parking area in front of the little concrete picnic table and stopped the car. When she got out, only then did he push up, away from the bike and out of his nonchalant pose. The light from the single utility pole high up threw a harsh circle over them and their vehicles.

Quinn opened the saddlebag on his bike, pulled out a neatly folded blanket and carried it under one arm. He took her hand and led her past the picnic table and stone barbecue pit to the shadows, past the circle of light and into the almost pitch-dark shelter of the woods just beyond. He stopped and spread out the blanket over the thin carpet of pine needles on the ground as she stood silently, watching him.

Without a word, he took her hand and pulled her down beside

him in the almost-complete darkness. His hands moved quickly as he reached behind her with practiced assurance and unzipped her dress, slipping it down off her shoulders and down her arms. Becky made a small sound.

Quinn framed her face with his long fingers, and his lips brushed across hers, igniting a flame inside her. "You okay with this, Becky?" he whispered.

She took a quivering breath, inhaling the smell of him and feeling the heat radiating from his body. Tentatively, she reached up and circled his neck with her arms. "Yes," she whispered, and the word unleashed the onslaught of his gentle attack.

His hands moved over her, efficiently removing and discarding the remaining barriers of her clothing. At the same time, his fingers conducted a lust-arousing exploration of her body. They moved over her breasts, fingertips teasing her nipples into hardness before they moved downward, tracing a path over her stomach. They hesitated before they slipped inside the elastic of her panties, caressing the edge of her patch of wiry curls. He tantalizingly barely made contact there before he slid the silky garment down her long legs and over her feet.

Becky's hands moved to the front of his shirt as he rose back up over her; she fumbled with it, wanting to feel the contact of flesh on flesh. He let out a low laugh, reared up on his knees, and stripped the shirt up and off his body as she lay back, her naked body palely visible in the near darkness, her arms reaching up toward him. He paused to unzip and lower his jeans, and Becky's questing hand caught and grasped his erection.

"Not yet!" he said hoarsely, removing her hand and lowering his head to nip and suckle at the hardening buds of her nipples. His hand slid between her legs, and his fingers parted her, delving and gently exploring inside her folds.

She gasped, and her body stiffened when he captured the tiny bud of her clitoris between two fingers and began to stroke and fondle it. Becky began to thrash about, but he pinned her beneath his body, his mouth closing over hers, his tongue possessing and demanding.

She felt her slick wetness against his fingers as they worked inside her. His mouth continued to claim and possess hers, sending waves of sensation through her. Becky felt her entire body surrendering under the insistent mastery of his questing lips and tongue. When she moaned into the ravishment of his mouth, he stretched out his free hand, searching for his discarded pants in the darkness.

She felt his erection throbbing, rock hard and hot, pressed against her body. Finally, his questing fingers stilled, apparently finding what he had sought in his jeans pocket, and he raised his body away from hers just long enough to rip open the packet and roll the condom over himself. He moved his body down between her legs, spreading them wide, the fingers of one hand still moving inside her, unrelentingly keeping her just on the edge of release.

He entered her in one long, heart-stopping thrust as she parted and then clenched around him. She was panting and grasping at his sweat-slick shoulders as he plunged into her deeply and repeatedly. He pushed his hand between where their bodies joined, forcing his fingers up and inside her. He found and touched her swollen clit as he continued to ram into her, and she went over. Her body clutched and undulated in its orgasm, even as he let go and exploded into his own climax. Then he lowered himself onto her.

Several minutes passed before either moved. Finally, Quinn raised his head an inch or so. "You okay?" he murmured.

Becky simply tightened her arms to draw him closer.

After that night, they began seeing each other regularly. On Sunday afternoons, he roared up to her house on his Harley; she hopped up behind him, and they rode out of town, stopping to buy a bag of sandwiches and an icy six-pack. They ended up somewhere secluded along a back road on the blanket he kept in his saddlebag, their limbs entwined. On rare occasions, they took in a movie in the neighboring town on an evening when Quinn wasn't so exhausted after his fourteen-hour workdays that all he wanted was a long shower and bed.

In the weeks that followed, they really got to know each other. He began to open up to her, confiding that he had left the marines with a few thousand dollars saved up and a dream of owning a business of his own. Hired immediately upon his return by Hugh Thompson, who was hard at work building his own fledgling construction company, Quinn had fit right into that world with his brawn and quick intelligence. Within a short period, Hugh had recognized the local need for someone with know-how and the ability in the earth-moving area of the construction field. And Hugh, his boss and mentor, had supported and encouraged him as he invested his nest egg in a used backhoe and an even older dump truck. Almost immediately thereafter, Quinn had discovered a nice piece of property that was for sale, eight acres with a nice, wide highway frontage. He recognized it would be the perfect place for him to establish his new venture.

But the banks didn't agree and flatly turned him down for the needed loan. That was when Hugh Thompson stepped up for him, cosigning his loan so he could get the money he needed for the land, two or three additional pieces of equipment, and operating cash for a trio of workers to be hired. Quinn knew Hugh was stretching himself financially to support him, and this made him doubly determined not to let his friend down. Success was the only option Quinn felt he had. He threw himself into the demands of his work, operating the heavy equipment by day, then planning and doing paperwork and sales calls when darkness fell, when he could no longer be outside.

Becky became a familiar figure at the work site, driving up

around sunset with a box of food and cold drinks for Quinn and his tiny crew. Quinn would stop the backhoe and climb down to meet her at the edge of the site, shirtless, his muscular chest gleaming with perspiration under the covering of tats she loved to run her fingers over. He would smile and give her a sweat-salty kiss before he took the box of food from her and signaled to his men that it was dinner break time.

None of this went unnoticed, of course. It was a small town, whose main entertainment sometimes seemed to be a thorough discussion of the lives of its residents. So when these two became a couple, people nodded knowingly. It seemed apt that this head-strong couple would match.

The Smiths were a long-established family in town; four generations had lived there, intermingling and contributing to the growth and establishment of the town. Most recently, Becky's father, Herman, had purchased their house on Pine Street as a young man and lived there with her mother until he deserted them when they were still small girls, creating a scandal that probably had contributed to her mother's delicate health and her early death. The family had always been faithful church members, and when Becky, hardly larger than a toddler, had stood up in front of the congregation and belted out her angelic vocals, the whole congregation had responded with a possessive smile filled with pride in her achievement. But when that small girl grew up and, as a high school senior, started singing on the weekends at a nearby disreputable roadhouse, she had created a stir of talk in Phillips and encouraged the pitying looks given to the frail single mother who was trying so hard to maintain control of her headstrong daughter.

The Cavanaughs, on the other hand, had been a quiet couple, who owned a small house just off the highway about two miles north of town. Employed by the railroad, Clyde Cavanaugh had tragically died in his early thirties, leaving behind his dour, straitlaced wife, Marion, and a small son. The pension she had received from her husband's death was adequate to cover her living expenses if she was careful and frugal, and Marion certainly was that—and to a fault. Their small son quickly became the center of Marion's universe. Quinn was a lively, outgoing boy, full of curiosity and intelligence, getting into all kinds of scrapes. He loved anything with a motor, preferably one that gave him speed and an exciting ride. He grew to be movie star handsome, lithe and muscular; his mother was convinced that he could do no wrong.

Upon graduation from high school, Becky's older sister, Clara, had dutifully gone to work, finding a job at the town diner. Their mother had never been a strong woman, and her uncertain health put a burden of responsibility on her two girls to do their share in helping to pay the bills. When Becky got her job at Jake's club and was making more money working two nights a week than her sister did during her six days at the diner, she was met with a certain amount of resentment on Clara's part; and their mother was mortified by the idea of her daughter singing in a place described as seedy in its best moments. This caused more than a little discord in the household, but Becky was doing what she loved, and she was determined to continue, regardless of any objections her family might raise. She dreamed of becoming a famous singer; a star.

Now, years afterward, Becky sighed, remembering. *We might have made it*, she thought. She and Quinn might have made a life together. The girls she worked with had cast sidelong looks of longing at Quinn when he made his infrequent visits to Jake's to catch her performance, and they let Becky know he was the best-looking man they had ever seen. And he was an accomplished and wonderful lover; she certainly had no complaints in that department. But everything changed one Saturday night that winter.

Becky had been chatting with some of the band members just before it was time for the club to open when Jerry Fox, their lead guitarist, came hurrying in, his face ruddy from the cold. "You're not going to believe who's here," he said, excitement glittering in his eyes.

"Who?" Duncan Royal, the drummer, asked.

"Tripp Thomas!"

"Tripp Thomas? Really?" exclaimed Randy Whitt, the stage manager, who was there every night to take care of the lighting and equipment.

"Who's that?" Becky asked idly.

"Who's that?" Jerry repeated incredulously. "Just the finest guitarist I ever heard play! He came by to visit me today, and I talked him into coming by the club. I left him back in Jake's office. He stopped in to say hello, and I introduced him to Jake."

"How do you know Tripp Thomas?" asked Duncan.

"I met him out in Nashville once. I was trying out for a gig out there, and he already worked for the band where I was trying to get hired. We got to talking, had a couple of beers." Jerry shrugged. "I didn't get that job, but he and I became friends anyway. He happened to be in this area today, and he looked me up. I invited him to come in with me tonight. I took him by to meet Jake. I think Jake's going to ask him to do a guest appearance tonight—play a number or two with the band."

"That would be great!" said Duncan. He looked at Becky. "Tripp Thomas is pretty well known in the country music circuit," he told her. "He's close to being a star in his own right."

"Oh," said Becky in a small voice. "I never heard of him."

Just then Jake came walking across the room, accompanied by another man.

Becky eyed the stranger curiously. Of medium height—maybe even an inch or so shorter than she was, Becky judged—the man emitted an air of confidence and authority as he walked closer. Dark-brown hair fell almost to his shoulders with a slight up curl at the ends; his eyes were gleaming darkly under thick, bushy brows, and his lips curved up in a sexy, knowing smile. Broad shoulders and long arms gave him a powerful, muscular appearance.

They halted in front of the small group. Jake made a gesture toward the man. "This here's Tripp Thomas," he said. "He's agreed to make a guest appearance onstage, playing with the band during the main performance tonight. These yahoos are the ones you'll be playing with—oh, an' this is Becky Smith. She's one of my opening singers."

The man threw a quick, cursory glance over them. "Hello, boys! I already know ol' Jerry here." His voice was low and gravelly. He took another step closer to Becky, those dark eyes taking her in with a scrutiny that missed very little. He gave a low whistle. "Hel-lo, Becky," he said.

"Hello," she said, extending her hand. He captured it and raised it to his lips, his intense gaze never wavering. As his soft lips brushed her fingertips, Becky felt a flash of something like an electric shock.

"Wait'll you hear her sing," Jake was saying. "She's pretty good."

Becky felt a flush heat her cheeks. Praise in any form from Jake was rare indeed. She looked up through her eyelashes toward Tripp and felt an almost physical blow as their eyes locked.

"I—I need to go get ready for my number," she managed and escaped on legs that had turned to water, her breath hitching. *What's wrong with you?* she chided herself as, her hands shaking, she zipped herself into her slinky on-stage dress and high heels.

When she glided up to the microphone after her introduction, every atom of her being was aware of Tripp's shadowy figure, which she immediately spotted leaning lazily back against the bar. The place was about half full, the usual buzz of conversations and the clink of bottles suddenly overwhelmed by the musicians striking up the first notes of her opening number. As she eased from one song into the next, she tried to give her attention to the tables of customers, about half of whom were actually listening to her; but her eyes kept being pulled back to Tripp. He stood unmoving, his casual pose belying the intensity with which he seemed to drink in her every note.

Her trio of songs done, she slid past Lucy, the other opener, who was being introduced. She circled around and walked up to Tripp at the end of the bar.

"Well?" Becky gave him a tentative smile as he turned to her. "How was I?"

He stood there for a long moment, staring at her. Taking in a long breath, he reached out, his calloused fingertips brushing roughly against her cheek. "Darlin', you got the voice of an angel," he said softly.

Becky felt a flush of pleasure run through her. "Really? You think so?"

"I know so," he said in that gravelly voice. "You got the makings of a star. A real star."

Becky's hungry heart gobbled up his words. She gazed at him, transfixed.

"I gotta get you out of here," he mumbled. "You need to be listened to by somebody who can help you."

Becky laughed self-consciously. "How's that gonna happen?"

"Leave that to me. I know people." His expression was dead serious. "I need to get you out to Nashville."

Becky's heart slammed in her chest. *Nashville! My heart's desire!*

Lucy's set was coming to an end. "Hey, Tripp," the bartender reminded him. "You need to get your guitar and get ready to go up on stage. There's a ten-minute break, then we start the headliner show. You're going to be in on that."

"You're going to stick around, aren't you?" he asked Becky.

"Yeah, I'll be here. I gotta sing again after you guys finish. Lucy and I do another set to close," she reminded him. *Like you could pry me away*!

"Okay. I gotta go out to my car and get my guitar. We'll perform, and I'll talk to you some more after that."

"Sure," said Becky, watching him thread his way toward the exit. "I'll be here." The smattering of applause throughout the room signaled the end of Lucy's performance.

Tripp was announced, just before the headliner, as a visiting performer "straight here from Nashville." When the band played an impromptu number halfway through the main performance, letting Tripp do a long solo, Becky watched, transfixed, as he bent over his instrument. The most amazing music flowed from beneath his fingers. She wasn't the only one who thought so; the whole place quieted as he played, and he looked up, grinning broadly when the room erupted into a prolonged burst of applause, foot stomping, and whistles when he finished. He bowed his head in acknowledgment.

The headliner's final number seemed anticlimactic. Becky almost felt sorry for the woman, hearing the smattering of applause she got as Becky hurried to the dressing room to touch up her makeup.

He was waiting when she left the stage for the second time that night. He took her arm and hustled her into the little hallway that led back toward the dressing rooms, pressing her back against the wall, invading her space.

"Oh, my God," Becky breathed, her eyes even with his, his breath warming her; she smelled the odor of tobacco smoke and whiskey against her face. "That was fantastic! You play ..." She struggled for words. "You sounded so great! I never heard anybody play like that before."

"Oh, yeah?" He grinned, his teeth big and square behind his lips. He leaned even nearer. "Well, I feel the same way about you, darlin'. God! You're sexy! And with that voice! I wanna take you outta here, get you set up to sing somewhere important, maybe even cut a record. I could be your manager, and with that voice of yours ..." He trailed off, and his hand came up to cup her breast, caressing it through the slick fabric of her dress. "Man! What a pair we'd be! Just like Sonny and Cher, only on the country scene. What do you think about that?"

Becky's heart was pounding. "I ... I ..." was all she could manage.

He reached into his pocket and pulled out a key attached to a fob. "Tell you what. Let me go say goodbye to Jerry and get outta here. I'm staying at the Cloverleaf Motel out on the High Point highway. Room 206. It's about five miles from here." He pressed the key into her hand. "Meet me there in an hour. We got a lot to talk about."

Becky stood speechlessly as he brushed his lips across hers, grinned at her, and left her standing there. Numbly, heart still beating furiously, she opened the door to the tiny dressing room she and Lucy shared and went inside.

An hour later, Becky pulled her mother's old car into a parking spot beside the Cloverleaf Motel. She shut off the motor, unsure why she had come. Was this guy for real? What was she doing here all alone, meeting a guy she'd never seen before? She looked up and down the long, painted brick side of the building. It was very quiet. A few windows showed light behind venetian blinds, but the narrow concrete porch running alongside seemed benign enough, lighted by a fixture every ten feet or so, jutting out of the building, even with the tops of the doorways. The big, brass numbers on the doors were clearly lit and legible.

Her eyes fell on the one marked 206. She bit her lip and swung her legs out of the car, closing the door and carefully locking it.

She walked up to the door, the key clutched tightly in her hand. But instead of inserting the key into the lock, she raised her fist and knocked.

The door swung open almost immediately. Tripp stood here, backlit by a lamp on the table by the bed behind him. He was barefoot, wearing his faded jeans. A T-shirt stretched tightly over his broad chest, dark hair peeking out over the vee of the neckline. His face lit up. "You came," he said softly, pulling the door open wider. "Come on in."

Becky stared around the room as the door clicked shut behind her. Tripp had turned away. "Let me fix us a drink," he said A moment later, he turned back, thrusting one of the plastic throwaway tumblers that came with the room toward her. It was half filled with an amber liquid. She took it.

He raised one to his lips and sipped. "Let's toast," he said, touching his cup to hers. "Here's to a long and prosperous partnership!"

Becky moved at last. Her limbs felt numb and robotlike as she raised the drink to her lips and took a sip, watching him. The fiery liquor burned its way down her throat as she swallowed, and she felt her eyes filling with tears.

Tripp circled her as she stood there, his eyes taking her in. Becky took another small sip, uncomfortable under his scrutiny. She shut her eyes briefly. This time the drink began to warm her as it spread downward into her stomach. He set his drink down on the end table and reached for her. Becky took a step backward, but he just took the glass from her hand and set it beside his. He smiled.

"Don't be afraid, darlin'," he crooned. "I meant every word I said to you. You've got the voice of an angel." He put his hand on her arm and urged her over toward the edge of the neatly made bed. "Maybe a very naughty angel"—he grinned—"but an angel nevertheless."

Her legs encountered the edge of the bed, and she sat down heavily. He sank down beside her, gently running his hand up and down her arm. "Jerry told you who I am?" he asked.

Becky nodded.

"Well, I'm set to go on tour the week after next. It's a worldwide tour," he added proudly. "Do you know who the headliner is?" He named a well-known country star, and Becky gasped.

"You're playing for *him?*"

Tripp nodded. "I am. But here's what's going to happen. When I get back to Nashville, I'm going to talk to some people I know, and I'm coming back here to get you. I'm taking you out there, and with that voice of yours, it's a no-brainer. I'm going to see to it that you're a country star. I want to be your manager, Becky. Are you good with that?"

Wide eyed, Becky nodded.

He leaned forward, and his lips brushed against hers, then moved to cover her mouth. "Oh," said Becky as his arms went around her, and he drew her to him. She felt another of the electric jolts she'd felt the first time he touched her back in the bar as his lips moved against hers, and his tongue probed for entrance.

He drew her back up to her feet, and his hands moved all over her body. "You feel this too, Becky. I know you do … come on, darlin'. Let me make you mine. Let's seal our deal right now."

Her hands rose to push against him in a token show of resistance, but his lips left her mouth and seared a path down her neck, while his hands were under her shirt in the back, busily unhooking the catch of her bra. They came around her body under the loosened garment, cupping and kneading her breasts as she felt her head go backward, exposing her throat to his mouth and tongue. His thumbs worked on her nipples, hardening the tips under his calloused fingertips, and Becky felt a gush of wetness in her crotch.

He tugged her shirt up over her head and down the cascade of her long hair. Any resistance she had left faded under the onslaught of his hands, and suddenly she found herself naked beneath them. He urged her backward onto the top of the bed and quickly stripped the clothes from his body. Becky's eyes widened as he lowered himself beside her on the bed. He was *huge*. His hands were between her legs, urging her legs apart.

"Wait!" she cried, pushing at him. "What are you doing? Don't you need to put on some protection?"

He paused and looked at her with a quick laugh. "Don't need it. Had my little nip and tuck years ago. Don't worry, darlin', I'm shooting blanks."

Becky looked back at him, feeling a mix of relief and doubt; but his busy hands had her gasping within seconds. He slid inside her, so deep that she cried out half in pleasure, half in pain as he filled her. A few strokes later, he ejected and eased himself down beside her, panting.

Becky lay trapped, her body half under him, waiting for him to breathe normally again. She eased her body from beneath him and planted a kiss on his lips, inching away toward the side of the bed.

His long arm reached out and pulled her back. "Where do you think you're going?" he asked, his dark eyes gleaming in the lamplight.

"I—I need to get on home," Becky said.

"Oh, no, you don't," he said, and something in his voice made her heart begin to pound again, this time with a touch of alarm.

He laughed. "We're not finished here. In fact, we've barely begun. That was just to take the edge off. Now we can get down to business."

He looked into her eyes. "I'm going to put my mark on you tonight. I'm going to make you mine!" His lips came down on hers again, this time with a possessive mastery that left her weak. His fingers ran over the softness of her belly, the calloused fingertips whispering against her skin as they moved over her.

He lifted his head and grinned down at her, lifting his hand in front of her face he wriggled his fingers. "They say I've got magic fingers," he told her. "And that's not just on my guitar!" He moved that hand between her legs, and she instinctively parted them as he began to stroke her.

True to his promise, her body was soon arching in response to him. She cried out as he brought her to orgasm and then teased her into another within an unbelievably short time. The third time, she grasped at him, sweaty and mewing her need.

He was hard again and rolled her on top of him, his hands on her hips. He lifted her to slide up and down his length, watching her hair fly about and her breasts bob in time with the strokes until they both came with gasps and wordless cries.

He seemed insatiable. Becky dozed off, weak and replete, only to be awakened again by his questing mouth or fingers somewhere on her body, reawakening her sensitive nerve endings into a response. And she would find herself shivering, grasping for him, and whimpering with want.

When she opened her eyes again, something felt different. The tumbled bed beside her was empty, and she heard a toilet flush. Sitting up, she winced. Her entire body felt sore and blissfully abused. "What time is it?" she asked as Tripp walked back into the room.

He paused and looked down at his wristwatch on the table. "Half past seven."

"Oh, my God!" Becky sprang out of bed. "It's morning! I've been out all night. My mama is going to kill me."

"Relax," he said, moving to slip his arm around her waist. "We'll get a shower, go get some coffee. Tell her you spent the night with a girlfriend or something."

Becky took a breath. "I guess I could tell her that," she admitted. Her lips curved. "But she'll be so pissed. I've got her car, and she won't have a way to get to church."

Tripp threw back his head and laughed. "Come on, let's get in the shower," he said. "Maybe you'll like it if I soap you up good. I know just the place to make you all slippery."

It was a long shower, complete with more sex. Becky felt like she could barely walk when he escorted her out to her car. She had firmly turned down his offer of coffee and breakfast, telling him she was really going to be in trouble if she didn't get home soon.

She rolled down the window as she sat behind the wheel, and he leaned forward to give her one last kiss. "When is it you have to leave on your tour?" she asked.

"Right away. We're scheduled to take off a week from next Wednesday."

"Will I see you again before you leave?"

"Tell you what," he said. "There's a ton of things I have to get done before we leave on the tour. But I'll make a special trip back here next Saturday night. I'll see you at the club."

"All right!" Becky gave him a tremulous smile and pulled out of her parking spot. Looking in the rearview mirror as she pulled out onto the highway, she saw him standing there, his hand raised in a goodbye wave, as she started home.

Becky watched the door of Jake's club anxiously as the hours dragged past the next Saturday night. The headliner was almost finished, and she would be on stage for her closing in a matter of minutes. *Where is he?* Anxiety began to eat at her. She had believed every word Tripp spoke, had given herself to him body and soul. The promises he had made, the dreams he had sparked in her, had seemed so real.

Now her mind was in a turmoil of worry and doubt. Had he had an accident while coming here? Was his body lying mangled beside the roadside somewhere? There was no way—no way! —he would just fail to show up, not after what they had shared. Her face burned when she thought about the things they had done to each other, things she had never before done with any man, the helpless need she had showed him as he played her body the way he played his guitar.

He'll be here, she assured herself as she took the stage. She sang and left the stage to be replaced by Lucy. She paced as Lucy finished her set and joined her back in the dressing room, where they pulled on their jeans, sweaters, and jackets. As the last of the stragglers were encouraged out the door after the last call, she finally accepted the bitter truth. He wasn't coming; all his big talk and the dreams he'd spun had been just a ploy to get her in the sack, and she'd fallen for it hook, line and sinker.

She beat the steering wheel in anger and frustration as she headed back toward Phillips, tears streaming down her face. She wasn't sure which was worse—her embarrassment and anger at being made a fool of or the death of the little flame of hope she'd allowed to spring up inside her while listening to him talk about making her a star.

Becky turned off the road, her headlights switched off. She parked the car near the roadside under a big maple tree and walked the short distance to the darkened house. Quietly she approached a side window and, reaching up, rapped on the glass. Nothing happened, so she rapped again. There was a movement of the curtains inside, and Quinn pushed up the window, peering out at her.

"What the hell, Becky?" he said quietly. "What are you doing here in the middle of the night?"

"Oh, Quinn! I just needed to see you."

He stared down at her face for a long moment as she looked back up at him. "All right. Come around to the front door, and I'll let you in. Be quiet, though. You don't want to wake my mother." He stepped back and pulled the window back down.

She crossed the front porch and heard the click of a lock; the front door swung open. He stood there dressed only in a pair of briefs as she hurried inside and threw her arms around him, absorbing the heat of him. He disengaged her arms from around his neck and gave her a little tug. "Sh. Come on back to my room," he whispered, pulling her with him.

He closed the door to his bedroom firmly before slipping his arms loosely around her. "What's the matter, Becky? What's wrong?"

"N-nothing," she stammered. "I just needed to see you tonight. Real bad." She was shivering.

She sensed rather than saw his frown in the darkness. "Are you sure nothing's wrong?" he asked.

"No." She pressed her body against him. "I just got so lonesome driving back from work tonight. I knew I had to see you."

"You're cold."

"I know," she said coquettishly. "Maybe if I get under the covers with you and you hold me real tight, I'll get warm."

He glanced over his shoulder at the closed door. "Keep your voice down. I don't want to wake my mother. Becky, tell me the real reason you're here."

"I am telling you the real reason." She felt the tears spill out of her eyes and took a step closer, resting her face against his bare shoulder so he could feel the dampness. "Oh, Quinn, don't be mad at me. I really did just want to be with you tonight."

He sighed, but his arms came around her, and she relaxed against him. "I wasn't joking about being cold. Can I please just crawl in beside you under the covers for just a few minutes? Please?"

"All right. I guess so."

She slipped out of her coat and reached down and slipped off her shoes. He got into bed and held up the covers for her. She slid in beside him and pressed her body against his.

"I'm not prepared for anything tonight, Becky," she heard his voice murmur against her ear. "We used the last of my condoms last week when we were together, and I haven't made it back to the drugstore."

"That's all right," she told him. "Just hold me, okay? I just need you to hold me."

They lay there for a long time until Becky heard his breathing deepen into a soft snore. She reached down between them and un-snapped her jeans, beginning to work them down her legs an inch or two at a time, taking her time. When they were bunched around her ankles, she carefully maneuvered and pushed them down and off her feet. She hooked her thumbs in the elastic of her panties and worked them off as well.

Reaching down, she began to touch and fondle the growing lump she found under his knit briefs. As he swelled and lengthened under her touch, she became aware of the change in his breathing.

His hand captured her wrist. "What do you think you're doing, Becky?" he hissed in her ear.

"Oh, God, Quinn," she whispered. "You just make me so hot! I want you so much."

He rolled over against her, and his hand went to her naked hip. "I want you, too. But I told you. We don't have any protection."

"I don't care!" She guided his hand between her legs to touch her. "I just want you inside me, Quinn. Please! I want you so bad."

"Are you sure?" His fingers were dipping inside her, stroking and fondling.

"Yes!"

With a quick, smooth motion, he yanked his briefs down his long legs, discarding them, and rolled on top of her, pushing her legs wide. She made a sound that was half whimper, half ecstasy as he slid deep inside her, then began moving slowly and sensuously in and out, his measured breaths conveying his control and his desire to make this last.

Becky's legs crept into a tight grip around his waist as their coupling continued, and the ache inside her began to fade; she concentrated on making her pelvic muscles grip and release in rhythm with his strokes until suddenly he gave a muted groan, and she felt him jerk and buck inside her.

Slowly, Quinn lowered himself beside her. He pressed his forehead to hers. "You won't believe how I've dreamed of having you here in bed with me," he whispered, raining kisses across her face.

She stroked his hair and stared up into the darkness as he slipped into sleep.

Her eyes popped open with a start, and Becky couldn't remember where she was. She turned her head to see Quinn propped up on an elbow beside her, watching her.

"Good morning," he whispered, his eyes laughing at her confusion.

Becky's eyes flew to the window. It was still gray outside, but the first streaks of dawn had begun to light the sky. She pushed back the covers. "I need to leave," she said softly.

"Yeah," he sounded regretful. "You probably do. Get your things on, and I'll sneak you back out the front door."

Becky scrambled up and, grabbing her discarded clothes, located them beneath the covers. He regarded her with what looked like amusement. He swung out of bed and grabbed her, pulling her close. "Sorry about last night?" he asked.

She stopped still. "No." She looked him in the eye, giving him a small smile. "Are you sorry I interrupted your sleep?"

He chuckled. "Anytime."

She hastily got into her scattered clothes. She pulled on her coat, and he tiptoed with her to the front door. Opening it carefully, he gave her another of those sexy grins of his. "Take care driving home."

Becky simply gave him a nod and trotted off across the yard toward her car, which was parked down by the roadside.

Her mood dipped lower and lower the closer she got to the club on her drive to work the following Friday night. For the first time, she really didn't want to be here. Entering the building, Becky saw the place through new eyes—detached, impartial eyes. It was an old, seedy honky-tonk, dirty and nondescript, a gathering place for drunken, pleasure-seeking yahoos who sought only a few hours' cheap respite from a life of hard work and little hope for betterment. How had she ever viewed it as a first step toward a glamorous music career?

She choked back a bitter laugh as she snagged her pair of dresses from the back seat. What career? Here she was, just like her sister, who came home every night dead tired from carrying platters of high-cholesterol food all day long, deep in a rut in a road that led to nowhere except old age and whose only escape was death.

She made her way back to the tiny dressing room she shared with Lucy and hung the dresses on the metal rod provided for that use.

By the time Lucy came bustling in, all giddy and full of chatter about the new guy she'd met, Becky had her stage makeup on. She forced a smile and half listened, nodding in all the right places, as she slipped into the tight red sheath dress she wore for her first set.

Moses, the old, cotton-headed black pianist, was already at his place on the piano bench, noodling out a soft, jazzy tune as she stopped, just out of sight from the room, behind the bandstand. Becky had heard that Moses used to be a famous jazz pianist in New Orleans or somewhere like that. For the first time, Becky wondered what had happened to him, if what she had heard were true, and what chain of events had brought him to this backwater dive in the backwoods of North Carolina. The other musicians were filing in, getting ready to play. Everyone except Jerry Fox, that is. He was running late, as usual. She heard hurrying footsteps and saw Jerry rushing toward the stage.

Becky took a step backward as Jerry brushed past her, hurrying in and clutching his guitar case. He glanced at her as he passed, took another step forward, then stopped and snapped the fingers of his free hand.

Turning back, he leaned toward her. "Hey, Beck!" he said. "I totally forgot to tell you something last Saturday."

Becky frowned at him. "What?"

He smiled sheepishly. "Well, I have to admit, I came in kinda buzzed. Had a few drinks with ol' Tripp that afternoon before I came in, and it totally slipped my mind."

"What slipped your mind, Jerry?" Becky said impatiently.

"Oh, Tripp told me to tell you that he had to catch a flight out early Saturday evening and couldn't make it back here to see you. Y'see, some stuff came up about the tour. They called him from

Nashville, and he had to be back there earlier than he expected. So, he caught a flight back a day early."

Becky's breath caught, and she suddenly felt woozy.

"Sorry, I totally forgot to tell you," Jerry said. "Tripp made me swear I'd let you know that he had to leave but that he'd see you just as soon as they got back from the tour."

"You forgot? You forgot to tell me?" Becky felt a sudden wave of anger bring a flush to her cheeks.

He grimaced and gave a little shrug. "Sorry." He turned around and walked over to his place on the stage.

"How long did he say he was going to be gone?" Becky called after him.

Jerry shrugged. "I dunno. He didn't say—a few months, I guess. It's a *world* tour."

Becky's mind reeled. She was torn between joyous relief and fury at Jerry's carelessness. *He didn't just leave,* she thought. *Tripp said he'd come back for me!*

She barely heard the band play a few bars to get the customers' attention before she was announced. Numbly, she stepped up, gave a big smile across the room, and automatically sailed into her opening lyrics.

Chapter Eight

"*What's the matter with* you?" Clara asked crossly, staring across the dinner table at Becky about a month later. Becky had been pushing her food around her plate listlessly, head down.

Becky looked up to see both her sister and mother staring at her. "Nothing," she said.

"What do you mean, nothing?" Clara persisted. "You ain't hardly touched your supper. You usually eat like a horse."

"Didn't I hear you throwing up in the bathroom this morning?" her mother put in. "Are you coming down with something, Becky?"

She shook her head. "I just don't feel good," she said.

"You think maybe you picked up a virus? I wouldn't be surprised at anything you ran into, working in that awful club. There's no telling what all you come in contact with in that place," said her mother with a delicate, little shudder.

"Maybe I did pick up a bug," Becky admitted, pushing back her plate.

On Sunday she was standing by the mailbox near the driveway, waiting, when Quinn came rumbling up on his Harley. She hopped on behind him. "We need to go somewhere and talk," she said into his ear as he rolled out onto the street.

"Sure, babe," he responded.

They pulled up at the little picnic table at the exit off the interstate, which coincidentally was the place where they had stopped the first time they had sex. Becky got off the bike and walked over to the table. Quinn gave her a frowning look and followed.

"What's this about?" he asked, removing his helmet as he walked toward where she leaned her hip up against the table.

She looked up at him. "I'm pregnant," she blurted.

"What?" He gave her a hard, searching look.

"You heard me."

His lips tightened into a thin line. "Shit!"

"Yeah! That's what I think, too!" A slow swell of anger ran through her.

"You sure?"

"Of course, I'm sure!" She heard her voice rise shrilly. "I got a test kit from the drugstore yesterday," she said more calmly. "It turned pink! It was positive."

Quinn took a deep breath. "So, what are we going to do?" he asked.

"I don't know! You tell me!"

"Look!" His pale eyes blazed at her. "You drop this on me, right out of the blue, and expect me to come up with a plan ten seconds later?"

"One time!" she cried. "One lousy time we do it without a rubber, and I get caught."

"Yeah? Well, who was it who came to my bedroom? Who was it that said it would be okay?" he shot back. "You climbed into my bed, all hot and heavy, after I told you I didn't have any protection!"

They stood in silence, glaring at each other. Becky dropped her head and put her hands over her face. "My mama's going to have a shit fit when I tell her."

He laughed grimly. "I don't think mine's gonna be dancing in the streets either." He took a step closer and put his hand on her arm. "Look, do you want to find, you know, a place to get this taken care of?"

She raised her eyes. "Do you know where I could do that?" She stared at his face for a moment. "Well, I don't either. Besides … I—I'm not sure I could do that. It's a life, Quinn. It's a little baby."

Quinn sighed. "Okay," he said.

"Okay, what?" She glared at him.

"Okay, we'll get married. I'll marry you."

"Well, don't fall all over yourself being romantic."

He glared at her. "I don't see any candles or hear any soft music."

She covered her face again.

"Come on. I'll take you back home. I'll pick you up Monday morning, and we'll go see what we have to do about licenses and blood tests, whatever," he said in a flat voice.

Becky hesitated, then followed him back over to the bike just as he swung his leg over it. She numbly got up behind him and held onto his waist as he started up and swung back out onto the highway.

Now, years later, Becky's eyes burned as she glanced up at the kitchen clock again, remembering the way so many events had worked out. The next few months had been hell on earth for her. They had their little civil ceremony, and Quinn moved her things into his bedroom in the house with Quinn's mother, who acted as though she smelled something rotten every time she looked at her.

Becky continued to work for another month or so until her baby bump began to show; then she was stuck spending much of her time in the house with her mother-in-law as Quinn spent increasingly long hours working to keep his fledgling business going during the slow winter months.

Her mother had, indeed, had a fit when she heard the news, doing one of her familiar swooning acts, then lamented Becky's poor taste in choosing a "wild hoodlum" to bring into the family to whoever would listen. And the neighbors listened. Avidly.

Caught between his mother's cold disdain and Becky's hysterical complaining, Quinn stretched himself further into debt, coming up with a small down payment for a little house located near this mother's, which he and Becky moved into only a month before she gave birth. They had only the barest of bare necessities, but being away from Quinn's mother was such a blessing that Becky resolved never to utter a word of complaint. Ever.

Strangely, his mother was instantly captivated by their baby boy, whom they named Benjie; the angular, cold woman became an instant, adoring slave to the baby, cooing and humming as she held him. Becky could hardly believe her own eyes. This meant nothing, however, in her mother-in-law's attitude toward Becky. She still acted as though she were a queen subjected to being in the presence of a lowly peon or worse whenever they were in the same room.

The fight of the century occurred, however, on the day when Quinn came home, and Becky met him at the door with the news that she was going back to work at Jake's club.

"You're going to what?" Quinn yelled.

"I'm going to go back to work," she repeated. "It's just for two nights a week, exactly like I used to do, and we need the money."

"We don't need it that bad," he declared. "My business will really pick up over the summer. If you want something to do, you can come over to the office, answer the phone, and help me out with the paperwork. You could bring the baby with you."

"You know yourself that I'm no good at that kind of thing," she argued. "And besides, I'll be bringing home money for us at the club. With the monthly payments you've got on the equipment and the mortgage on the house, we really need the income." *And besides, I'm going crazy here*, she added to herself.

"What about Benjie?" he asked. "You've got a baby to look after. Benjie's barely two months old. What if I don't get home in time to watch him while you go chasing off down there?"

"Your mother will be happy to watch him until you get home," she answered. "I already asked her to."

He finally relented. Becky headed off that Friday night, both anxious and excited. If Quinn only knew what she had to do to get Jake to take her back, she thought with a tightening in her chest. If he ever found out what Jake had made her do …

She'd heard the rumors, of course. But Jake had always treated her respectfully enough. He knew she had a good voice, that quite a few customers came in just to hear her sing, and that she was a decent draw for his business. So, what happened when she visited the club to ask for her old job back took her totally by surprise.

"So, you wanna come back, do you?" Jake said, squinting up at her as he sat, leaning back in his chair behind his desk. "I guess you know what the entrance fee is for me to hire you back, don't you?"

"No, what?" Becky asked innocently. Butch, one of his bouncers, looked at her and sniggered.

"Why, it's real simple," Jake said in a mocking voice. "All you gotta do is come over here and put those pretty lips of yours where they'll do the most good." He shoved his chair back from the desk and unzipped his pants.

"You're kidding," Becky said, her mouth dropping open in shock as he reached into his pants and pulled out his flaccid member.

"Nope. You want the job or what?" He grinned at her as he grabbed and fondled himself. Butch leaned back against the wall, smirking and watching avidly.

"C'mon. You've got thirty seconds to decide. If you want the job, you get on your knees and make it good for me—nice and slow."

Frozen, Becky looked frantically from Jake to Butch, then back at Jake again.

"But ..." Becky whipped her head around, looking at Butch.

Jake frowned. "What?"

"Butch," whispered Becky.

Jack snorted. "Oh, never mind him. He likes to watch. Right, Butch?"

Butch let out an amused snort.

Becky turned her head back unbelievingly to stare at Jake. He made an impatient gesture. "You want the job or not?"

She hesitated before moving like a sleepwalker. Slowly she crept over in front of the chair and dropped to her knees.

Every time she thought about the event, her cheeks burned with mortification. If Quinn ever found out, she knew he'd kill Jake. And maybe her, too! But at least she was out of the house. At least she was singing again.

She had been greeted with catcalls and whistles, along with extended clapping, when she walked out onto the stage that first night. People remembered; people came to hear her. This fact filled her with a heady glow that almost overrode the bad taste from her recent experience in Jake's office. Conversations muted to the point that she could even hear the distinct clinks as bottles were being set down on the tables as she began to sing.

She was filled with a deep-seated yearning connection, a strange mix of something she couldn't quite put a name to, as her eyes roved over the indistinct blurs of faces in the dimly lit room. Faces turned up toward her to hear her. When she finished and the sound of applause reached her as she bowed and smiled, Becky felt that she had come home.

Chapter Nine

She had been back working for just over a month. Every weekend was a silent struggle of wills—the disapproval on her mother-in-law's dour face as she dropped off the baby, the grim acceptance with which Quinn took the little stack of bills she pushed into his hand. She did this when they met in the kitchen on Sunday mornings after she had been paid on Saturday night, his eyes like the surface of a frozen lake.

Becky hated the situation. But it was worth it, she reasoned, even if it was just for the few moments when the wonderful feeling swept through her as she stepped under the spotlight, and she heard the opening notes of her first song. The remainder of her week passed with the mind-numbing boredom of washing diapers, mopping floors, and cooking dinners for her husband. He was so tired that he didn't even seem to taste them before taking a shower and collapsing into a coma-like sleep. Meanwhile, she lay there and listened, waiting for the hacking cries that would come, calling her to climb out of bed to answer the demands of a hungry and wet baby.

One day she was standing just beyond the end of the bar, where a few steps backward would take her into the little hallway that led to the dressing rooms, listening to the headliner. In her opinion, the woman had all the talent of a squeaky door. Why she had been hired to stand up there and bombast her audience with a voice whose main attribute was volume was beyond Becky's compre-hension. Even the band members rolled their eyes behind her back and simply played mechanically for her. Becky was getting up her nerve to approach Jake and ask for a shot at the headliner slot. It might be the right time to make her play, she was thinking, when a pair of strong arms grabbed her from behind and she was yanked roughly back into the hallway.

She had just opened her mouth to scream when a mouth cov-ered hers, hot and demanding. Her arms were captured at her sides in a vicelike grip. She tried to yank her head back; her frantic eyes caught sight of the amused dark ones inches away, and she went limp with shock and recognition.

"Tripp!" she cried when his mouth finally released hers. She threw her arms around his neck when he released his grip on her. "Oh, my God, it's you. It really is you!" She felt rather than heard the rumbling chuckle as his chest pressed against hers.

"It's me, all right," he said, holding her so tight against him that she could barely breathe.

"What are you doing here? Is the tour over? When did you get back?" The questions tumbled over each other as she looked at him standing there, grinning lazily at her.

"Tell you all about it in just a little while," he said. "Ain't it about time for you to go on?"

Becky snapped back to reality. "Oh, yeah, it is," she said.

He gave her a little pat on the backside. "Tell you what. I'm gonna go out there, sit down, and get me a beer while I listen to my angel voice sing for me. Then we can have us a talk."

Becky nodded voicelessly and stepped aside as the headliner pushed past her on her way to the dressing rooms. She took her place offstage, just out of sight of the audience, as she heard herself being announced for her closing set. Automatically her lips curved up into a dazzling smile, and she stepped up to the mic. Her heart was pounding, and her hands shook as the band launched into her opening number and she began to sing.

Somehow, she finished her performance and left the stage, smiling and acknowledging the applause as onstage Lucy was announced and took the microphone for the closing number. Becky threaded her way through the tables until finally she spotted him at a table near the back, a curl of smoke rising from the cigarette in one hand, a beer bottle held loosely in the other.

"Hey." She slid into the chair next to him.

"Hey, yourself, pretty thing. Are you ready to get outta this place and start making some real bucks for a change?"

Becky laughed. "That sounds like something I could go for," she replied, thinking he was joking.

"Well, pack your bags! Have I got stuff to tell you!"

She looked at him. His casual posture was belied by the heated gleam in his eyes. "What are you talking about, Tripp?"

He leaned closer. "You won't believe who I met while I was on tour. You ever heard of Bud Wilson? I can see from your expression that you haven't. He's a bigwig record producer out of Chicago, with ties to New Orleans, Nashville, St. Looie, all the music hot spots. Well, guess who I worked with on my tour? None other than Bud Wilson's nephew, Charlie." He leaned back and looked expectantly at her.

"That's great, Tripp," Becky said, her forehead creasing in a frown.

He grinned at her. "You don't get it, do you? See, I made friends with Charlie, showed him a little trick or two on the guitar. He was real impressed. And he told me that his uncle is looking for some new talent out in Nashville."

"I still don't get it," said Becky.

"Charlie's our ticket in," Tripp said. "He's going to get us an introduction to his uncle." He snapped his fingers and gave his head a shake, grinning. "That's going to be it, sweetheart! I told

Charlie about you, and he passed the word on to his uncle, Bud. He can't wait to meet you. All you've got to do is sing for him, and it's a shoo-in for him to offer you a record contract. And that will be that!" Tripp leaned back in his chair, grinning broadly.

Becky's lips parted as what Tripp was telling her began to sink in. "Are you sure about all this?" she almost whispered.

"You betcha I'm sure! I told you I'd get you outta here, make you a big star! What do you think of ol' Tripp, now?"

"Oh, my God!" breathed Becky.

Tripp crushed out his cigarette. "When can we get started?" He gloated. "How long will it take you to get packed up to leave?"

"Oh, my God!" repeated Becky. Her hands flew up to cover her face. "Oh, no! Oh, no!"

"What's the matter?" asked Tripp. "I thought you'd be over the moon when I told you what I got set up."

"I am! Oh, God! I am! It's a dream come true." Her mouth twisted with dismay.

"That's what I thought you'd say! So, what's the matter, Becky?" His expression was puzzled as he regarded her.

"Oh, Tripp! I … there's something I have to tell you." Her head dropped, and her stomach clutched. "Something happened while you were gone."

"What happened? What is it?" Tripp asked, eyeing her with concern.

She winced, looking up at him through her lashes. "I—I got knocked up," she confessed.

She saw his sudden intake of breath. He slowly let it out again. He picked up the pack of cigarettes that lay in front of him on the table, shook one out. Putting it between his lips, he struck a match, lit it, and inhaled. Squinting at her through a cloud of smoke, he said, "You don't look pregnant. You took care of it, I presume."

"Sort of," she told him.

"Sort of, how?"

"I ... actually, I had the baby. I have a little baby boy."

He sat very still, staring at her. "Come again?"

Her fingers twisted together. "Yeah. You heard what I said."

Something moved behind his eyes. They went flat. "What happened, Becky?" His voice was quiet, too quiet.

"I—well, you remember how you said you'd be back here that next Saturday night after we, you know."

"Yeah. But I had to leave early. I sent word to you by Jerry."

"He didn't tell me. He forgot."

Becky watched him as full comprehension registered. "He didn't tell you?" Tripp's eyes blazed, and he let out a string of profanity, using phrases more imaginative than she'd ever before heard, ending with "That damn pothead!" He moved as though to rise out of his chair. Becky laid a hand on his arm.

"He finally remembered to tell me. He ended up telling me the next week. Tripp, please!"

He glowered at her as he sank back down onto his chair. "Okay. So how did that get you pregnant?"

"Well, that Saturday night, when you didn't show up and he didn't tell me why, I, I ... felt real bad. I thought you'd run out on me. So, I guess I ... well, I went to see somebody I'd been going out with."

"Oh, shit, Becky!"

"I know! I know!" She bit her lip and squirmed under his glare.

He closed his eyes. "So, you got pregnant."

Becky nodded miserably.

Tripp smoked his cigarette in silence. When it burned down, he ground it out on the tabletop. "Damn it, woman! I thought you knew how I felt about all this! I told you! I don't go around telling every woman I meet that ... damn it! This was special ... this was real! I took my time on all this. I've got everything all lined up, pretty as a picture. All I have to do is show up at the recording studio with you, and we're on our way. Now this! You're telling me that you've got a kid. What're we going to do with a kid hanging on to you? Goddamn!"

"Tripp."

He took another deep breath and reached out to where her hands were clasped together on the table. He covered them with his big hand. "Okay. It's okay. Let's think about this. We'll still make it work. It might slow us down a little bit, but we can still do it. With your voice … yeah. We can keep the kid in the background. It'll still work. So, let's go pick up the kid, and we'll be on our way." His mouth moved in what looked like a forced smile. "Don't worry, Becky. It'll work. We'll make it work."

Becky chewed on her lip and winced as she looked at him. "Tripp, that's not all."

His eyebrows flew up. "There's more?"

She nodded, her heart sinking.

"What in hell else could there be?" The frown was back, twisting his face.

"I'm married," she whispered.

"Son of a bitch!" His fist hit the tabletop. Around them, the people at adjoining tables were starting to stare. He glanced around, then lowered his voice to where the music covered their conversation. "You're married?" he asked incredulously.

"It was because of the baby!" Becky cried defensively. "It's not a real marriage. Not really," she added when Tripp just continued to stare at her in disbelief.

A waitress approached the table, looking inquiringly at the empty bottle in front of him; Tripp waved her away impatiently. After a long pause, he breathed in deeply, and his face slackened; its lines became more pronounced. "So, where does that leave us then?" he asked.

Becky looked at him helplessly.

"You wanna give up on this? You don't want to have a singing career? Is that what you're telling me?"

"No!" Becky cried.

"Do you want me to go talk to him—this husband of yours?" Tripp asked.

"No!" cried Becky. "No, no, no," she repeated, a picture of those two alpha males in the same room flooding her mind. One of them probably wouldn't leave that room standing, she realized, chill bumps rising on her arms. She rubbed her forearms unconsciously.

"What then?" Tripp growled. "Do I just leave you here and go back to Nashville alone? Forget all about the sweet deal I've got set up?"

"No," Becky moaned. Her head came up, and she looked at him, raw pleading in her eyes. "I want to go. Take me with you, Tripp. Please let me come with you."

"What about your baby? You wanna drag him along? Do you expect me to raise your kid? What are you asking me to do, Becky?" His face was hard again, forbidding.

"I don't know!"

"I don't think it's gonna work, Becky. It's hard to do something like this—build a career from scratch. You gotta be ready to move and move fast on a moment's notice. With a baby"—he shook his head—"I just don't know."

"What if ..." Becky almost whispered. "What if it was just me? What if I came by myself?"

Tripp spread his hands. "Hey! That'd be great. But how is that going to happen? How old is this kid of yours, anyway?"

"He's almost four months old." Becky took in air. "But he's used to staying with his grandmother some anyway. And his dad—" Her mouth twisted with bitterness at her words. "His *father* is always too tired to take me out anywhere, but he always has time to play with the baby, give him his bath every night, feed him his supper." Her face took on a distant look. "Maybe … maybe I could come back and get him later, after I make it big."

Tripp narrowed his eyes at her.

"Yeah! I could do that." She bit her lip. " I could always come back to get him, give him a better life when I become a star. I could do that, couldn't I, Tripp?" She looked pleadingly at him.

"How bad do you want this, Becky?" His voice sounded harsh. "How bad do you want a singing career?"

"Oh, God, Tripp! More than anything! You know how much I want to sing!"

He reached out and gripped her hand hard. "How bad, Becky? I need to know. Once we start, there's no turning back. It's all or nothing. How bad do you want it?"

Her eyes met his, unflinching. "Bad, Tripp. I want it bad."

"Okay, then. Here's how it's going to work. No tears, no whining! I ever see one ounce of regret, and I'll kick your ass back here so fast you won't know what hit you." His grip tightened, became painful. "You want it or not?"

Becky refused to flinch. "Yes."

The waitress came up to the table. Hesitantly she cleared her throat. "Last call," she said. "We're closing in a few minutes. You want another drink? Last call."

Tripp shook his head without so much as blinking, his eyes boring into Becky's. "You sure? You better be real sure, Becky. I mean it."

"I'm sure," said Becky.

Tripp stood, his grip still hard on her hand. He pulled a wad of bills out of his jeans pocket with his free hand and carelessly tossed them onto the table. Giving her a little yank, he pulled Becky to her feet. Another pull brought her unresistingly chest to chest with him. "Come back to my motel with me," he rumbled. She felt his hot breath against her face. Her knees almost buckled as a lurch of desire flashed through her.

"I ... I can't," she whispered, her mouth suddenly dry as ashes. "Maybe ... maybe I could just come by for a little while and then drive on home."

His hands grasped her forearms, rubbed up and down them possessively. "If you come to my room, you won't be going any-where else tonight," he said.

Her eyes closed for a second, and her breath left her. She gave herself a little shake. "I have to pack," she said in a rush. "I have to make ... arrangements." Her lips trembled. "Can I ... can I meet you tomorrow?"

He pushed her a few inches back, his hands like iron bands around her forearms. Again, his eyes bored into hers like stone. "I'll wait for you until one o'clock tomorrow. Not a minute later. If you're not there by one, I'm outta here. I'll be on an airplane, and you'll never see me again. Understood?"

"I'll be there," she insisted weakly. "Just tell me where you're staying. I'll be there by one o'clock tomorrow. I promise."

"You'd better!" He told her the name of his motel and the room number. "One o'clock," he repeated. He gave her a wry smile. "This sure ain't the way I expected to be spending my night." He walked away and left her standing there in the almost-empty room.

Chapter Ten

Becky started and looked up at the slow-moving hands of the kitchen clock again. Tense and edgy as she was, she could hardly believe she had almost dozed off, her head resting on her folded arms atop the kitchen table, lost in her memories. It was almost time for her to drive over to the diner. Becky couldn't imagine why Clara thought this was so important. She simply couldn't get her head around why her sister was putting such stock on their talking with Quinn's current wife. But she would give it a shot.

True, she didn't know the woman and had laid eyes on her for only a brief moment or so—and that while falsely representing herself. There was no reason in the world for Donna to do anything to help her.

Becky opened the refrigerator and poured herself a cold drink of water, her mind still in the past, remembering her final Saturday in North Carolina, which had been so long ago, yet it seemed like only yesterday.

In that long-ago time, when she had opened her eyes, Becky had been alone in bed. Creeping as silently as possible into the house the night before, she had slipped into bed beside Quinn, who had been snoring peacefully. But sleep didn't come to her for a long time.

It had been after three when she got home, which was normal

for her on her work nights. Usually she was tired, and sleep came quickly. Tonight, however, her brain was in overdrive. Fear and excitement warred inside her; her palms were clammy, and her heart pounded like a trip hammer. How could any human being have gotten into such a mess? If only Jerry had passed Tripp's message on to her like he was supposed to; if only she hadn't gone to Quinn for comfort when she thought Tripp had run out on her; if only he'd had had a damn rubber … if only, if only!

She switched positions, trying hard not to wake her husband. *Her husband*! Why had she rushed into this marriage? She could have had the baby without marrying him, but then she would have been the talk of the town—the town slut! They were probably the talk of the town anyway—or close to it.

Nashville! The magic city of her dreams—and Tripp had connections there. He could make her a star, or so he claimed. This was her big chance—her only chance. So what if she had to leave Quinn behind—and Benjie? Benjie, that sweet, innocent little thing. He hadn't asked to be brought into the world, and his happy, little gurgles made her heart almost stop when he looked up at her, reaching those pudgy, little arms up to her. How could she even think about going off and leaving him?

But how could she stay, knowing that she'd had a chance, a real chance, to reach for the stars? Hell, to be one of them—to be a star! Becky didn't know when it was that she finally slipped into a fitful sleep.

She jumped out of bed and hurried to see what time it was. Good Lord, it was already nine thirty. What was she going to do? The house was quiet. Quinn was gone, either off to where he had a job in process or over to the office to catch up on paperwork. He was gone—but for how long? Maybe all day, maybe not. She heard Benjie start making whimpering noises she knew would soon evolve into a full-throated demand. A bottle and a diaper change were in order no matter what else happened. Becky hurried to pick up her baby.

An hour later, the baby was dry and fed, and Becky had the contents of two dresser drawers and half the closet spread out over their unmade bed, sorting through them. She had dragged an ancient suitcase, the only one they owned, down from where it was stowed in the attic. It sat open on the floor beside the bed as she picked over her belongings, selecting which she thought would be suitable to take with her. When she could stuff nothing more into it and still be able to snap it closed, she hauled it out to the car and concealed it in the trunk.

Picking up a ballpoint pen and ripping a sheet of paper out of an old notebook, she began to try to explain herself to Quinn. Several attempts later, she simply wrote, "You need to pick up Benjie at your mother's. I can't do this anymore. Becky." Propping the note up at his place at the kitchen table, she gathered up some formula, diapers, and the baby, and headed outside. She put Benjie in his car seat and drove the short distance to her mother-in-law's house.

"We have a special rehearsal at the club today," she lied to the stern-faced woman, who met her at the door. "I have to be there. Quinn will pick Benjie up when he finishes working today." She put the car seat down and almost ran out of the house before she could change her mind.

Her hands were shaking so badly that she clutched the steering wheel more for support than to guide the car as she made her way down the highway. Her heart was pounding, and she was almost gasping for breath when she finally covered the several miles and pulled into the parking lot of the motel where Tripp had told her he was staying. She wiped her sweaty palms on the legs of her jeans as she got out and walked toward the numbered door. She knew it was almost noon and that she was ahead of the deadline he had given her, but anxiety had her stomach in knots, and her mouth was dry as she raised her fist and rapped on the door of his room.

After a heart-stopping moment, the door swung open, and Tripp stood there, rumpled, and unshaven, wearing only a pair of faded jeans, his chest and his feet bare. A slow grin began to light his face, and he stepped backward without a word. Becky's feet felt leaden and her rubbery legs barely supported her as she stepped inside the room.

An instant later, she felt herself being lifted and tossed across his tumbled bed. He landed half on top of her with a whoop before his hands were running all over her body, fumbling and ripping off her clothes. Her breath caught in her throat, and a laugh bubbled up inside her, along with a heated rush of lust as skin met skin, questing hands clutched, and their bodies entwined.

The sex was raw and intense. It was over within minutes, and he lay on top of her, panting, his eyes glittering. He gave a short, triumphant laugh as he cupped her breast with his hand and stared down at her. "I see you made up your mind," he said.

She moved her head up and down half an inch.

"You did right," he said, dropping his head, his mouth closing over her nipple. "Now, let me tell you hello like I wanted to last night."

"What about one o'clock?" asked Becky, closing her eyes as his tongue on her nipple sent ripples through her. "What about the airport?"

"I lied," he said, his mouth moving down her body. "We don't have to leave until four o'clock."

Chapter Eleven

Becky checked the clock again. It was time. She was exhausted, both from the tension of waiting for her meeting with Quinn's wife and from all her soul searching as she relived her memories. Rousing herself as the appointed time for her meeting finally arrived, she drove back downtown and parked as close as she could find a parking space.

Becky walked into the diner, looking around at the empty tables and booths; it was the slow time between the lunch crowd and early dinnertime. Clara was standing behind the counter, wiping it down with a wet cloth. She straightened and walked around to meet Becky halfway across the room. Clara made a motion of her head toward the row of booths along the side of the room closest to the back, and they headed toward them.

"Has she got here yet?" Becky asked nervously, looking around.

Clara shook her head. "It'll be a few minutes—it's now just three. She said she'll be here as soon as she can when school lets out," she said, indicating that Becky should take a seat in a booth about midway of the row.

"Are you sure she's gonna show?" Becky said nervously.

"She'll be here," Clara said calmly. "You want something to drink while we're waiting?"

Becky shook her head.

Clara looked at her through narrowed eyes. "You eat anything today?"

"No," said Becky.

"I'll bring you a soda. You want anything else? You really should have something on your stomach."

"I couldn't get anything to stay down," Becky told her.

The door opened, and a couple of young women came in and took one of the tables. "Let me see what they want," Clara said. "Be right back." She hurriedly took the orders, circled to the window behind the counter connecting the front to the kitchen, and came back, carrying several drinks on a tray. Depositing a pair of them in front of the women, she brought the others to the booth where Becky was sitting. "I told Al that he will have to take care of business for the next hour," she told Becky, sliding in beside her in the booth. "Told him I got some family business out here to discuss."

Becky raised her eyebrows. "Really?"

Clara's eyes twinkled. "Yeah. He knows better than to argue with me when he sees I really mean something."

Sure enough, when a lone man walked in and sat down at the counter, Al, the owner, came out of the kitchen and spoke briefly to him, then placed a cup of coffee and a piece of pie in front of him. Minutes later, he carried two plates out and placed them in front of the pair of women at the table without so much as a glance in Clara's direction.

The diner door opened again, and Becky saw Donna Cavanaugh walk in, looking around. She looked their way and headed toward them.

"Hey, Donna," said Clara as she reached them. "Sit down. I want you to meet my sister, Becky."

Donna slid into the booth, her eyes sweeping over Becky. "Hello," she said. "Your sister?" She raised her eyebrow. "I didn't know you had a sister, Clara." She looked back at Becky, and her eyes narrowed. "Say, didn't I see you a few days ago over at the school?"

Clara glanced at Becky. "I guess I need to clear some things up for you, Donna," she said when Becky didn't respond to Donna's comment. "This is my sister, Becky Smith. She used to be Becky Smith *Cavanaugh*, although she calls herself Becky Barnes now."

Donna's lips parted in surprise. "You're *that* Becky?" She gasped. "Are you telling me that you're Quinn's ex-wife?"

Clara nodded.

"I had no idea." Donna looked from one to the other. "Clara, I didn't know Quinn used to be married to your sister!"

Clara smiled grimly. "I didn't think that you did," she said.

"Quinn's never mentioned ..." Donna stopped, and the confusion in her eyes gave way to a guarded, expressionless look. "Okay," she said. She focused her attention on Becky. "What are we doing here, Becky? What do you want from me—from us?"

Becky's hand on the table fluttered. "I'm not here to cause trouble," she said.

"Well, I certainly should hope not!" said Donna, starting to rise.

"Wait, please," Clara put in. "Donna, please. Just hear her out. Just listen to her for five minutes, won't you?"

Donna frowned and gave Clara a hard look. "Okay." She settled back down stiffly. "Five minutes, Clara. This is because you're the one who's asking," she said, turning her gaze back to Becky. "Now what is it you want to say to me?"

Becky took a deep breath. "I know you probably haven't heard anything good about me," she said. "And I don't blame you for not wanting to have anything to do with me, but please believe me when I tell you that I'm not here to cause you or anybody you know any trouble."

"Then what *are* you here for?" Donna asked flatly. "Why are you here?"

Becky met her eyes steadily. "I wish I knew," she said. "All I really came here for was to see Benjie. I just wanted to see him with my own eyes and make sure he's ... all right."

"Benjie's fine."

"I know that! I know that he's probably a lot better off than he would have been if I'd been the one who raised him." Becky felt her eyes mist. "I just had to see him for myself. Surely you can understand that."

Donna shook her head slightly. "No, I don't understand. I don't understand you at all. I don't know how you could have left him in the first place."

"It was wrong," Becky admitted. "What I did ... the way I left ... was terrible and wrong. But what I did can't be changed now. I just did what I felt like I had to do at the time. But surely you can understand how much I needed to see him."

Donna's mouth twisted. "Now? You want to see him now? Why now? After all these years?"

"Do you think I've ever stopped thinking about him?"

"I don't know. Have you?"

Becky leaned forward. "Please, Donna. Give me a little bit of a break here."

Donna continued to stare at her. "What do you really want, Becky?" she repeated in an unrelenting voice.

"I don't know," Becky twisted her hands together helplessly. "All I want to do is just to see Benjie, talk to him. I just want to let him know who I am and maybe ask him to forgive me."

"I don't think that would be wise," said Donna.

Becky looked at her imploringly. "What does he know about me?" she asked. "Has he ever asked about me? What have you told him about his mother?"

"I haven't ever told him anything," Donna said, but her eyes softened slightly. "I know that Quinn has said that he used to ask questions sometimes. He just told him that his mother had to go away but that it didn't mean that it had anything to do with him, that it wasn't because of anything Benjie did. He told him that it didn't mean that she—you—didn't love him."

"Well, thank God for that much at least," said Becky.

"It had nothing to do with you. All Quinn wanted was for Benjie to feel secure and loved," said Donna. "He didn't want Benjie to ever think he had anything to do with you not being here."

The tears that had pooled in Becky's eyes finally trickled out. "Quinn's a good guy," she said softly. "He always was a wonderful father, right from day one."

"I know that," said Donna dryly. "He's a wonderful father."

Becky absently rubbed her fingertips under her eyes, wiping away the tears. "Is there any way that I can talk to Benjie? Please! I really need to. You have no idea how much I need to."

Donna was shaking her head. "I don't see how," she said. "I don't see how it could possibly be a good idea, anyway. No." She shook her head firmly. "I don't want him upset. It's better if he never sees you."

Becky covered her face with her hands. "Oh, God!"

"Why don't you just go home?" said Donna. "Go find someone and start a family of your own and forget about Benjie! You went away and left him, so stay away. Go and have another little baby if you want a child!"

"I can't do that!" whispered Becky.

"Why not?"

She dropped her hands and looked at Donna through her tears. "Because I had to have a hysterectomy," she said. "Benjie is the only child I'll ever have!"

Clara looked at her in surprise. "You didn't tell me that," she said. "I didn't know that, Becky."

Becky nodded, her expression bleak.

"When?" persisted her sister. "When did you have it?"

"A few years ago. What does it matter?"

She turned away from her sister's shocked face and looked back at Donna. For the first time, Becky saw what looked like just a glimmer of sympathy in Donna's big, expressive eyes. "So, you're saying that all you want to do is meet Benjie, talk to him, and let him know who you are?" Donna asked softly.

"Yes! That's all. I wouldn't do something to disrupt his life for anything. Please believe me when I tell you that!" Becky stretched her hands across the table imploringly.

Donna regarded her speculatively.

"I know he's happy. I know that!" cried Becky. "I'm telling you the truth. I don't want to upset him. All I want is just a chance to let him know who I am. Please. Oh, please."

Donna sat silently, her gaze steady on Becky's face. Finally, she sighed. "I'll talk to Quinn," she said softly. She held up her hand when Becky started to speak. "That's all I can promise! I'll talk to him."

"That's all we ask," Clara said quickly.

"I'll let you know what we decide," said Donna. "Where can I get in touch with you? Are you at Clara's?"

"Yes!" said Becky. "Thank you, Donna. Thank you so much."

"Don't thank me yet," she said, getting out of the booth. "But I'll talk to Quinn."

Becky turned and looked at Clara as Donna walked out of the diner. "What do you think?"

Clara gave a little half shrug. Her head made a little jerk; she pursed her lips. "Mm-hmm, I think she'll give it a try," she allowed. "But I wouldn't count on much. Quinn's a hard man, and you did hurt him, leaving them like that. You hurt him an awful lot." She sighed deeply. "We'll see. Donna has a good heart. She'll try to do what's right." Clara turned her attention to Becky. "Now, how about you? I know you haven't had anything to eat today, and you need something. What can I bring you?"

"Do you have anything here that isn't fried, coated in mayo, or smothered in either gravy or melted cheese?"

"How about I bring you a chef salad with dressing on the side? You need to eat."

"Way on the side," said Becky. "And forget about the strips of cheese as well."

Clara gave her a little mocking salute and hurried away in the direction of the kitchen, detouring to stop by another table whose occupants had just arrived.

Becky was mindlessly stirring the remains of the ice in her soda when Clara set a filled plate in front of her. Becky gave a brief smile. "Thanks, sis."

Clara leaned forward, bringing her face close to Becky's, and keeping her voice low. "Why didn't you tell me you'd had a hysterectomy? That's pretty major," she said.

"I don't know." Becky picked up her fork. "Maybe I wasn't sure you'd be interested in hearing my troubles."

"I'm your sister!" Clara glanced around. She lowered her voice again. "I may not be rich and famous, but I am family. I do care."

"I realize that." Becky speared a hunk of iceberg lettuce. "I guess I just didn't want to talk about it."

Clara slid in across from her in the booth. "Was Tripp with you when it happened?" she asked. "Was he supportive?"

Becky chewed on a bit of carrot. "Oh, yeah. I couldn't have asked anybody to have been better to me."

"That's good."

"You just don't get it about Tripp and me," Becky told her. "We never got married, but we're closer and more to each other than most of the married couples I've ever seen. And he's my manager as well. He takes care of all the bookings and the money. He's been good to me and *for* me."

"Yeah? Well, how come you showed up here so broke that you had to go back to work for that Jake character again the minute you got here?"

Becky lowered her eyes. "I told you that Tripp left to go on his road tour. I had a lot of time on my hands, and I didn't have a lot of things to do to fill it. Most of the people I know had to do with work—the people in the bands and all the ones who produced the shows, like that. I've been out of work, so I don't know a lot of people around me where we live now.

"Everybody I knew was off somewhere, working, "she admitted. "I'm not a rising star who's twenty years old anymore. My records haven't hit like the first one did. And Tripp's a good, solid musician, too. Pretty well known. He can make good money playing. So, when I hit this last dry spell, he began looking for some gigs of his own to tide us over. That's why Tripp hired out to go on tour."

She was silent for a moment. "See, that's why I ended up in the apartment all by myself with too much time on my hands." Her eyes came up, flashing green. "My career's not over—not by a long shot. I just need the right record. I haven't found it yet, but I will! I just need to find the right song, that's all."

"I know you will," Clara assured her. "How come you two never got married, though? Have some kids?"

"It didn't seem like it was necessary to get married. In fact, it was better for my career for me to be single. And Tripp can't have any kids anyway. He got that fixed a long time before we met."

"Well, then, I guess your hysterectomy wasn't such a big deal for you then, after all."

"Oh, yeah it was!" Becky leaned forward, her eyes glowing with emotion. "They took away my *choice*. Don't you see? I might not have planned to have another kid, but it still was my choice, *my decision.*" She put a clasped fist against her chest. Her brow furrowed. "After that, it was over. No more questions about it. I'd never be a mother. I couldn't."

Clara's lips tightened. "I'm sorry, Becky," she murmured.

"That's when I started thinking about Benjie," Becky confessed. "After I had my surgery, I started wondering about him—what he looked like, what he was doing. Picturing him in my mind, wondering how he was turning out. That's when I knew that I had to see him again."

"Oh, Becky!"

Becky jammed another forkful of lettuce into her mouth, chewed on it hard.

Clara glanced around the room. "Look, I gotta go. I gotta take care of these customers. You eat your salad, and I'll be back in a few minutes, okay?"

Becky nodded and took another bite. As she ate, her thoughts wandered back to another time years ago, back in Nashville, the night that changed everything.

There wasn't much warning, Becky remembered. She'd had a nice gig that night, and she had been happy to get it. It was minutes before she was supposed to go on stage that she felt a hot gush of wetness between her legs. She hurried to the little half bath off her dressing room, sat down on the toilet, and reached for the roll of tissue. She said a curse word when she wiped herself, saw the blood on the paper, looked down, and noticed how red the water in the commode was. Her periods had always been heavy, but this was getting ridiculous.

She found the box and inserted a new tampon. "Coming!" she called in response to the heavy warning knock on her dressing room door just at that very moment. Pulling her tight dress back down over her hips, she slipped her feet into her stilettos and crossed the dressing room. She heard the wave of applause engulf her as she stepped under the blinding lights onstage. Tossing back her mane of hair and giving her audience a big smile, she sailed into her opening number.

The lightheadedness hit her about mid performance. Her mouth felt wooden, and the lights danced across her field of vision as she went through the familiar lyrics. Finally, she finished the last number and made her little bow as the applause rose in waves around her. As she turned around to walk offstage, her legs seemed to become boneless, refusing to hold her up, and everything went black.

When she opened her eyes again, she realized she was lying on a hard surface that smelled of starch and crackled loudly when she moved. She saw Tripp's face hovering over hers, his eyes dark with concern, the lines beside his mouth etched even deeper than she remembered.

"What happened?" she tried to ask, but no sound came out of her dry lips.

His mouth was moving. "Can you hear me?" she heard him say from far off in the distance. She closed her eyes just for a moment.

She opened them again to a world filled with pain. Harsh waves of it swept over her unrelentingly, carrying her off with it. She heard someone moaning and crying out. Just as she realized the voice was hers, she had to scrunch her eyes shut tight again as an especially bad surge of pain hit her, and the world disappeared again.

She heard voices around her. Something jarred the surface she was lying on, and she cried out at the sudden avalanche of pain. More oblivion.

She tried to lick her lips—so dry and chapped. Opening her eyelids just a crack, she became aware of the bright light around her, which made her eyes water. She squeezed them shut again. Someone grasped her hand—a big, warm, gentle clasp that made her feel better somehow. She slit her eyes and tried to focus.

"So, are you finally awake, darlin'?" Tripp's gravelly voice rumbled from somewhere nearby.

"Water," she whispered.

She felt the wonderful sensation of crushed ice pieces being pushed against her parched lips. Nothing had ever felt so good. She sucked at them greedily.

"That's enough," Tripp told her. "Go back to sleep now. I'm here." A warm hand enfolded hers.

When she surfaced again, the pain had changed to a dull throb all over her body. The room was darker now. She sensed rather than saw him move beside her when her eyes fluttered open.

"Hey," she whispered.

"You feelin' better?"

She closed her eyes briefly. "I guess. What happened to me, Tripp?"

"You collapsed last night while coming off the stage at the show."

"I don't remember."

"Well, I sure do. I've never been as scared in my life as I was when we loaded you up in that ambulance and brought you here."

"Can I have a drink of water?" She heard the soft gurgle as he poured some from a Styrofoam pitcher into a cup and held it near her face, pressing the end of a bendable straw between her lips. She took a big sip and would have taken more, but he pulled it away.

"Better take it easy," he said. "You don't wanna be sick."

"I hurt. What did they do to me?"

He paused. "You were hemorrhaging blood. It just started pouring out of you. The doctor had to do an emergency hysterectomy."

A chill of horror ran through her. Becky's breath caught as what he said registered in her mind. "Oh, no," she said.

He took her hand. "It had to be done, darlin'. You were bleeding out."

"But—why?"

"They said your uterus was just full of fibroids, and that's what was making you bleed so bad. I dunno. That's what the doctor said."

"Did they … did they take everything out?"

His hand tightened on hers. "Just your uterus, the ovaries, all the baby-making stuff. It won't affect anything else."

The door opened, and a nurse bustled in. "I see our patient's awake and talking," she said. "But she needs to rest." She brushed past Tripp and efficiently pulled aside the stiff sheet, and a quick sting on the outside of her thigh told Becky she had been given a shot. The nurse looked up at Tripp as she quickly pulled the sheet up to cover Becky's torso. "Why don't you run along and let your wife get some sleep? She'll be off to dreamland in a few minutes, and you can come back to see her again in the morning. We'll take good care of her for you. You need some rest yourself."

After a hesitation, Tripp nodded and bent over to plant a kiss on her cheek. "I'll see you tomorrow, okay?" Becky heard him say as everything began to grow fuzzy again.

She was sitting propped up, with the head of her bed elevated, when he approached the bedside at midmorning the next day. She eyed him without speaking as he walked up, a vase of flowers clutched in one hand. He set it down on the wide windowsill near her bed beside a huge potted plant already resting there.

"Who sent this?" he asked, reaching for the little envelope stuck in the plant on a plastic holder.

"The club where I was performing," she answered dully. "Maybe they were afraid I'd sue them."

He cut his eyes around to her. When she didn't say more, he moved over to stand beside her. "What's the matter?" he said. "Are you hurting?"

"A little bit," she said. "They got me out of bed and made me walk to the bathroom."

He nodded. "Do you want me to have them get you more pain medicine?"

She shook her head, avoiding his eyes.

"Well, I had to run the gauntlet this morning, coming into the hospital. Reporters," he told her when she glanced quickly up at him. "You made the news." He made a face. "Reporters *and* the tabloids. You know— 'Singer Collapses after Her Performance.'" He sighed. "The public wants to know what happened."

"I can't do an interview," she said with a note of panic in her voice.

"That's all taken care of," he reassured her. "I told them you were going to be fine and that you were resting comfortably. They seemed to be satisfied and went away."

Becky's face crumpled, and silent tears began to stream down her face.

"Here now! What's the matter?"

"Oh, Tripp! I'm not a woman anymore!"

He reached out, cupping her chin in his big hand and turning her face toward him. "What are you talking about? Nothing has changed. You're every bit as much of a woman as you've ever been!"

"No, I'm not!" she said through sobs.

"Hush, now. Of course, you are." He pulled a tissue out of the little box on the bed stand and wiped her face tenderly. He hesitated, then moved his hand under the stiff, white sheet. He slipped it down to her legs and brought it up between her thighs, beneath the short hospital gown she wore, below the thickly padded dressing across her abdomen.

"Tripp, what are you doing?"

"Sh-h," he said, working his fingers up between her legs to where they joined, softly caressing her folds. He slid the tip of his index finger inside her and began moving it gently.

"What are you doing? Stop it, Tripp. Someone's going to come in!"

"No, they won't," he said as his fingers parted her and began stroking and fondling her, seeking. She gave an involuntary gasp as his fingertip touched the slick little nub inside her.

A tiny flicker of sensation radiated from his fingertip out into her abused and sore body. "Tripp!" she said reprovingly, her eyes widening above the tracks of tears on her cheeks.

"Hush, baby," he said, his finger barely moving, eyes intent on her face. "Relax. Just relax."

A small wave of pleasant warmth began to spread through her, and her muscles tightened around his probing finger. She felt her nipples tighten. The caresses continued, and she closed her eyes. Gently, slowly his finger moved until a small shudder ran through her.

She opened her eyes to see him looking down at her, his feelings warming his eyes. He bent his head, and tenderly his lips caressed hers as he slipped his hand away and removed it from under the stiff sheet. "I told you that you were still a woman," he said softly against her mouth. "You've still got the important stuff."

Never had she loved him more.

Chapter Twelve

Becky was sitting in her sister's small living room. Clara had been home from work just long enough to change out of her waitress uniform and into sweatpants and a loose shirt. She came into the front room and switched on the TV to a sitcom, while Becky leafed idly through the latest issue of *People* magazine.

The telephone in the hallway rang, and Clara got up and went to answer it. Try as she might, Becky couldn't make out who was on the other end of the call by Clara's short, one-word responses. She strained to hear the conversation over the sounds of voices and laughter on the TV program.

Minutes later, Clara came back into the room and sat back down in one of the pair of armchairs facing the TV. "That was Donna," she said.

Becky put down the magazine, her full attention focused on Clara. "What did she say?"

"She's talked to Quinn. He's not happy at all, not with any of this," Clara told her. "But he did finally agree that they needed to tell Benjie who you are, that you're here in town, and see if he wants to meet you."

"All right!" cried Becky. "That's good, isn't it?"

Clara inclined her head in a slight nod. "I guess so."

"When can I see him?" Becky said.

"We don't know yet," Clara told her. "Quinn and Donna are going to tell Benjie tonight. It's up to him then—it's going to be Benjie's decision."

"Well, he'll say he wants to see me," Becky said confidently. She eyed her sister. "Why wouldn't he?" she added.

"I don't know. But don't get your hopes up too high. Think about it. He has no memory of you, and suddenly he's being told that his birth mother is in town." Clara pursed her lips and shook her head.

"He'll be curious if nothing else," Becky said. "I can't imagine him saying no."

Clara gave her a flat look. "We'll just have to wait and see," she said.

"Why are you being so negative?" Becky cried.

"I'm not. I'm just telling you that things don't always turn out the way we want them to. Not for some of us, anyway."

Becky narrowed her eyes. "What do you mean?"

"Look at you! Becky, I'm just trying to tell you that you may not always get things the way you want. You're too used to always having everything go your way. Maybe it won't this time around."

"I don't know what you're talking about. I don't always get things to go my way."

Clara threw up her hands. "Oh, yes, you do! When we were back in high school, you got to pick and choose. You could have dated any boy who struck your fancy. It gave you great pleasure to cut out somebody who really liked some boy, to flirt with him and date him once, just to show her that you could, and then you'd lose interest, dump him, and move on to the next!"

"Why, I did no such thing."

"Sure, you did! Then, when Quinn came back from the marines, every woman in this town who was under the age of twenty-five and single was giving him sidelong looks, hoping to catch his eye. What did you do? I don't know how you did it, but you caught his interest, so you were the one he was dating. Then you got pregnant, and that was it! He married you.

"But even that didn't satisfy you. Along came Tripp, and he was your ticket to getting out of here and having a career in Nashville. So, too bad, Quinn! You take off and leave with Tripp, just like that. Not just Quinn, but you left that sweet, helpless, little baby behind as well. Did you think he'd get in your way?" Clara gave her a condemning look. "Now you've decided that you want to be in Benjie's life. So here you are again, trying to get close to him."

Becky's face had paled, and her mouth hung open. "I can't believe that you think that way about me."

Clara's hands were shaking, and she looked appalled at her own words. "It wasn't just me, Becky. A lot of people were saying that very thing."

"Oh, my God, Clara. You're jealous of me!"

"No, Becky, I'm not. I'm just trying to let you see how people looked at the way you acted. Maybe that's not the way it was. But you've got to realize that not everybody sees things the way you do. Not everybody will think bad of Quinn if he doesn't want you to have anything to do with Benjie."

Becky's face crumpled. "I just want to see my baby! I'm not the kind of person that you just said I was. I never meant to hurt people."

Clara walked over, sank beside her on the sofa, and put her arm around her sister's shoulder as she began to sob.

"I know, Becky. I don't think you're a mean person. I don't believe you try to hurt people. I'm just trying to make you understand that maybe this time around, things won't go the way you want them to. You have to be prepared for that to maybe be what happens."

"No, no, no," said Becky. "I have to talk to him. I need to."

Clara rubbed her back. "Becky," she said, "sometimes in life you don't always get a 'happily ever after.'"

Becky was so bored and antsy that she couldn't keep still. Moreover, after what Clara had said to her the other night, she was scared. There wasn't anybody she really knew here, she reflected, and nothing to occupy her most of the time. At least Clara had a job to go to, she thought resentfully, something to eat up the endless hours until they heard from Donna—until she found out whether her son wanted to meet his mother.

It crossed her mind that she could get in her car, drive down to Winston-Salem, and do a little shopping there, but she rejected the idea. She wasn't in the mood, and besides, she really didn't have the money to make her way through the high-end shops she preferred, selecting whatever caught her attention.

Things had changed since she was the big country star, who could walk into Nashville stores, be recognized, and have the staff falling over backward to please her every whim. No longer did she carry a credit card she could whip out when a cute pair of shoes caught her eye or she found a blouse she could order in every color. She thought wistfully of the mall at Green Hills—having her driver drop her off on one of the rare days when her schedule allowed her time for a carefree day of browsing and spending.

She walked outside Clara's little house and aimlessly prowled the backyard. Here she was, right back where she'd started, she reflected, leaning against the trunk of the big tree that used to have a swing hanging down. There she and Clara had spent endless hours whiling away the days of their childhood. She shut her eyes and felt a wave of self-pity engulf her, the sound of the insistent ringing of the phone inside the house not registering at first. When the sound finally penetrated her awareness, she raced inside.

She grabbed up the receiver. "Hello! Hello!" she said as the dial tone hummed in her ear. "Damn it all!" She slammed the receiver back down, only to pick it up again and dial the number for the diner.

"Did you just try to call me?" she asked when Clara finally came on the line.

Her shoulders slumped when she heard the negative reply. "No, no, I was out in the yard, and the phone rang. I just missed a call, and I thought it might have been you. I guess you haven't heard from Donna? Okay. Just checking." Becky hung up again, feeling more depressed than before.

It was Wednesday afternoon before they heard anything. Clara called Becky from the diner. "Donna called me," she related.

Becky's heart lurched before falling back down into her stomach. "Finally! What did she say? Did Benjie say he wants to meet me?"

"Yes," replied Clara. "But hold on. There are a lot of strings attached," she cautioned.

"What do you mean?"

Clara gave a short bark of laughter. "Remember, we're dealing with Donna Cavanaugh! I should have predicted that she'd have a bunch of rules and regulations."

Becky was almost spitting with impatience. "What rules and regulations? I just want to know if they're going to let me talk to my boy."

"Calm down!" Clara said. "Yes, you can talk to him. But Donna is going to be there the whole time, listening to every word and supervising the whole conversation."

"That's fair enough," Becky agreed after a moment of thought. "When? When can I see him?"

"This afternoon, if you want."

"Of course, I want." Becky heard her voice rise. She took a deep breath. "When and where?"

"Donna said she and Benjie will meet you at those benches in the little area outside the library at three thirty, after school lets out. She said it might be a little chilly."

"I don't care!" interrupted Becky. "Tell her I'll be there."

"Okay. I'll call her back and let her know. She said to tell you that they'll get up and leave if you say anything to upset him."

"I'm not planning on saying anything to upset him!" cried Becky.

"I know it. But she said to tell you that, and I have. Now, let me call her back and tell her you'll be there at three thirty."

Becky hung up the phone, trembling. She leaned back against the wall, her stomach roiling. This was her only chance! She had to make it good. What could she say to him? Her little boy!

Becky drove up to Main Street and parked just down from the library. She anxiously checked the time; it was a quarter past three. After a momentary hesitation, she opened her car door and stood.

The late November afternoon was sunny, but the slight breeze carried a nip; she adjusted her coat collar higher and walked along the sidewalk until she was even with the small parklike area occupying the space adjacent to the building. The area was cheerfully welcoming during the summer with its lush flower beds along the winding path under three sheltering trees, but today it looked inhospitable; the flower beds were bare of vegetation, the slim tangle of azalea bush limbs behind them bare sticks. No one occupied the wood-and-metal benches alongside the path, above which hung the stark tree limbs. Their leaves having long since fallen, scarcely acknowledged the passing breath of wind.

Nearby, the tall, lighted library windows displayed racks of books in their military rows inside. The silence was broken only by the occasional passage of traffic down the street.

Becky shivered, feeling very alone as she sank on one of the pair of benches. She chose the one that afforded the best view of anyone passing by on the sidewalk; she slid over into the corner next to the metal armrest and placed her tote bag beside her, feeling both conspicuous and anxious.

For long moments there was no sign of anyone else around, outside of the passage of the occasinal street traffic. Then there came the whisper of unhurried footsteps on the concrete sidewalk.

Donna Cavanaugh was approaching, accompanied by a young, adolescent boy. Benjie! Becky's heart leaped and began to pound. *God, he is so beautiful!* Her eyes drank him in from the top of his tousled head down over the oversized sweatshirt and faded jeans to the scuffed, well-worn tennis shoes. She felt her lips curve in a happy smile.

Donna halted at the juncture where the path met the sidewalk, and Benjie stopped just behind her, his head bowed, ostentatiously looking down at his feet while sneaking glances at her.

Becky rose to her feet as Donna regarded her, her face unsmiling. "Hello, Becky," she said across the ten feet or so separating them.

"Thank you for allowing this, Donna," said Becky. "You don't know how much I appreciate—"

"We're here," Donna interrupted her, her expression flinty, "not because Quinn and I feel this is a good idea but because I convinced him that it was the right thing for us to do under the circumstances. But you better remember that I am here to monitor what is said and done, and if this becomes upsetting to Benjie or if I think this is headed in the wrong direction, it stops instantly, and we leave. Is that clear to you?"

"Of course," said Becky, taken aback. "I have no intention of doing or saying anything that will cause problems." She gestured toward the second bench. "Won't you both sit down?"

"I think I'll just stand right here," said Donna stiffly.

"Fine." Becky finally permitted herself to take a good look at Benjie, who stood there so uncomfortably, his head still bowed; but she could see that he was watching her carefully from his lowered eyes. She could hardly restrain herself from rushing over to him and throwing her arms around him. Instead, she gave him a big smile and gestured to the bench where she had been sitting. "Hello, Benjie," she said softly. "Do you want to come sit here beside me so we can talk?"

He gave a small head shake.

"Okay," she said, sinking back down onto the bench, her eyes fixed on him. "Did they tell you who I am?"

He stole a look at Donna, then back to her and nodded.

"Did they tell you I'm your mother?" Her voice trembled as she spoke.

His big, hazel eyes finally met hers. "You left my dad and me." The mumbled accusation hit her like a blow, and she felt the sting of tears.

"That's right," she said. "But I'd like to try to explain to you why I did that ... why I felt I had to do that. Will you let me try to explain it to you?" She held her breath as he stared straight at her. After a pause, he nodded, his eyes never faltering. She felt as though those eyes, direct and accusing, were looking straight into her very soul.

Becky took a deep breath. "It's very complicated, Benjie," she said. "But ever since I was a little girl, I wanted to be a singer. I wanted to do that more than anything you can imagine. Can you understand that?" She looked at him imploringly.

He didn't respond, but she saw that he was listening intently to her, drinking in every word.

"I wanted to be a singer … to stand up behind a microphone on a stage and have big audiences listen to me sing. I wanted to make records and have people listen to me sing on the radio. But there wasn't an opportunity for me to do that and live here in Phillips. There were no places here where people would come to hear me sing and no recording studios or people who were in the music business. In other words, if I wanted to become a country singer, I had to go live someplace else—and the best place for me to do that was in Nashville, Tennessee. That's where the country music business is. That's where it's done."

He was looking at her and frowning, but he was still listening. She suddenly changed direction. "What do you like to do most of all in the whole wide world?" she asked, looking straight at him.

"I dunno," he mumbled.

"Do you like to play sports or something like that? What sport do you like to play?" she asked him insistently.

"I dunno. Baseball, I guess."

"Baseball. Okay. Is that the thing you like to do best of all?"

"I guess. But I like it when my dad and I go up in his plane. He taught me to fly, and I'm going to get my license when I'm old enough. I like that."

Bingo! thought Becky. She opened her mouth to try another question, but Benjie beat her to it.

"You say you're my mother, but you went off and left my dad and me." His voice was filled with hurt. "You never even talked to us again."

Becky took a deep breath. "Yes. Yes, that's true."

"Why did you do that?"

Her mouth twisted into a grimace. "That was a mistake," she said softly. "I know now that I shouldn't have done that."

"But you did," he said. "If you had to go somewhere else, why didn't you take us with you?"

"Oh, Benjie! I'm so sorry." She looked at his stricken face, even as she saw Donna take a protective step forward from the corner of her eye. "I didn't mean to hurt you! But I didn't see a way to do that." She thought fast. "Let me try to tell you how it was. Can I do that?" She half rose as Benjie stared at her accusingly. "Please?"

"What?" He sounded exactly like what he was—a very hurt and sullen teenager.

Becky held up a cautioning hand as Donna looked as though she might intervene. "Benjie, what if ... what if you had told a friend of yours that you would throw baseballs with him ... to practice, right? What if, right before you were about to go out and throw baseballs with your friend, your dad came up to you and said, 'Benjie, let's go up flying.' You'd take off and go flying with your dad, right?"

"I guess so," said Benjie.

"That wouldn't mean that you didn't still like your friend, right? It would just mean that you wanted to fly more than you wanted to throw baseballs. Am I right?"

"I guess so," Benjie mumbled again.

"So, your friend shouldn't be hurt because you'd rather go flying instead of throwing baseballs with him, right?" Becky said triumphantly.

Benjie raised his eyes to look directly at her.

"See, Benjie?" She held up her hands toward him, palms raised. "That's sort of the way it was for me. I wanted to be a singer more than anything. I had to go and try, even if I couldn't take you with me right that minute. That didn't mean I didn't love you! Do you understand what I'm trying to tell you?"

He stared at her. "I guess," he said finally. "But why didn't you call us, or something?"

Becky dropped her eyes from that reproachful gaze. Tears stung, but she forced herself to look at him again. "I was afraid," she whispered finally. "I...just was scared to."

His stare was unrelenting. He looked at her for what seemed like an eternity before the tense line of his lips eased slightly, and he took a breath. His eyes shifted away. "Okay," he said so softly that she barely heard him.

She closed her eyes for a second with relief. "So, tell me, Benjie," she said. "Do *you* like to sing? Or play an instrument? Do you like music?" She swiped her fingers across her face to wipe away the tears.

One side of his mouth turned up a fraction of an inch. "I like to play the drums," he told her.

"Really!"

"Yeah." He took a step closer.

"Are you in a band?"

He nodded. "Sort of. We don't have a real band until I get to high school, but we have a little group that's kind of like a little band. The music director from the high school comes in once a week to teach us."

"That's wonderful! That sounds real good." Becky leaned toward him, looking up at him. "And you're learning to play the drums there? And you like it?"

He nodded.

"I wish I could hear you play sometime."

He gave her a shy smile. "There's a program we're putting on. We're playing this Saturday afternoon over at the school auditorium if you'd like to come hear us."

"I'd love it!" cried Becky. "I'll be there. What time?"

"Four o'clock," said Benjie.

"Benjie," Donna said, "I think we should say goodbye for now. The two of you can talk again another day, but right now we need to go get Sammy and Amy Lynne and get on home. I think this is enough for all of us to think about for this time."

She looked at Becky. "You can come and watch him play at their program on Saturday if you want to. That would be all right. As for anything further after that, we'll have to wait and see."

Becky got up and looked at Donna. "Thank you," she said.

Donna nodded. "Come on, Benjie," she said, and Benjie turned and fell into step beside her as they walked away.

Becky hugged herself. She felt battered, but her heart soared with hope. She closed her eyes. *This went well*, she thought, *really, really well!*

Filled with a mix of sadness, adrenaline, and happy excitement, instead of going toward her car, Becky turned right and walked the two blocks over to the diner. She needed to share the news with someone. She pushed open the door and walked into the almost-empty eatery, her eyes sweeping over the empty tables. Clara came hurrying toward her as she slid into an empty wall booth.

"How did it go?" Clara asked, her eyes reflecting her worry.

"Pretty good, I think." Becky permitted herself the smile she had been suppressing.

Clara visibly relaxed. "Thank heavens."

"Can you get a cup of coffee or something and sit down with me so I can tell you all about it?" asked Becky.

Clara looked around the room. "You bet, I can. I want to hear this."

When she returned with two steaming mugs, Becky related the whole conversation as best as she could.

"You don't know how happy I am to hear that it went as good as it did," Clara told her and absently rubbed the back of her neck as she took a sip of coffee. "You say that Benjie told you he was having a band thing this weekend, and he asked you to come? What did Donna say to that?"

"Nothing! I mean, she didn't say anything against it. In fact, she actually told me it would be all right if I wanted to come to watch it."

"Wow," said Clara.

"I know," said Becky. "I guess all I have to do is avoid sitting anywhere close to Quinn." The two sisters exchanged rueful smiles.

"No, really," said Clara. "If Benjie told you about his band recital and you said you'd go, you have to be there."

"Oh, I know it," said Becky. "By telling me about it, he was giving me a chance. He was reaching out to include me in his life. There's no way in the world I can miss it now."

"Just so you understand that," said Clara. "Really understand it, I mean."

"Oh, you better believe that I do," replied Becky.

Chapter Thirteen

Two days later, Becky played her first set on Friday evening to a full house; oh, there were a few empty chairs in the smoke-filled room, but for all intents and purposes, it was a full house. The applause was generous, accented with a few catcalls and whistles, as she turned and stepped down off the stage.

She smiled. This was good; Jake was going to be happy with the turnout tonight. The second show was always more crowded than the first, so maybe tonight they would have to turn people away, which made her look good, very good.

Susanna, the little blonde, was onstage. Becky listened to the music, punctuated by bursts of applause, as she changed into her second-act dress and heels. She sat down and refreshed her makeup.

Then it was time for her second set. She peered out toward the audience as she was being announced. She had been right; it looked like a standing-room-only crowd out there. The band began playing "Tarnished Rose," her signature hit, and she stepped into the spotlight to a wave of applause. The band had to repeat the opening bars because the clapping continued unabated for longer than usual. She gave her audience her most brilliant smile and launched into the familiar lyrics.

What a great evening, she thought as she left the stage for her second time tonight, flushed with satisfaction.

She took two steps into the little hallway toward her dressing room when a pair of strong arms seized her, one yanking her back against a sturdy, muscular body. A calloused hand clapped over her mouth, pulling her head back and warm breath hissed against her ear.

"What in the *hell* are you doing here?" was whispered fiercely into the hair behind her ear.

Becky's heart gave a leap of fear and began to pound. Her whole body stiffened. The arms around her felt like steel bands; she couldn't move. Even her head was held in place so she couldn't see her captor, and the big hand clasped so tightly on her mouth that she couldn't make a sound.

He took a step forward, then another, forcing her toward the doorway to her dressing room. One push against the unlatched door sent it flying inward into the dark, little closet of a room, and they were inside. The whole thing happened so quickly—the space of a single breath inhaled greedily over the big, bruising finger just touching the bottom of her nose.

Becky's legs felt like wet noodles as she was propelled forward, and her stomach clutched in panic. Simultaneously the door was kicked shut, and the hand left her mouth long enough to click on the overhead light. She blinked in the flood of light as she whipped around to face the man behind her. He stood like a figure of stone in front of her only avenue of escape. Her mouth dropped open as recognition flooded through her.

"Tripp!" she whispered, her lips numb and slow to move.

His face was a mask of fury, dark eyes glittering beneath the brushy brows, lips drawn back in a tight grimace, revealing his big square teeth. A new wave of panic ran through her, turning her muscles to mush. She stared at him, immobile.

His lips moved. "I've been trying to find you for days," he said, his voice a low, menacing rumble.

She took in a shuddering breath, her fear dissolving. "I'm right here."

He gave a flickering glance around before impaling her again with his dark gaze. "I see where you are," he said scornfully. "I got you out of this shithole once. How many times am I going to have to do that?" A note of pleading appeared in his frosty tone. "Becky, why on earth would you come back *here*?"

"I—I needed the money," she whispered. "I ran out of cash. Our account was empty, and I couldn't get hold of you." A surge of anger ran through her.

He groaned, and a stream of curses left his lips. "My bad, angel! We got paid. I had my check in my wallet, but it was during a really tight part of the tour. We'd play, pack up, and get back on the bus to the next town. We'd catch a couple of hours' sleep, then have to get off the bus at the next stop and set up for our next performance. I didn't have time to look for a Wells Fargo bank to put the money in our account. Same thing would happen the next day, and I'm sorry—I just sort of forgot to deposit the money for a while."

Becky stared at him. "I ran out of money. I panicked."

He did not speak; guilt and appeal written all over his face.

"I was all alone. I couldn't reach you."

"Becky—"

"You know how I get when I'm by myself, without you."

He nodded. "Yeah. You think too much."

"I was all alone," she repeated.

"I said I was sorry, darlin'. But the apartment rent was paid up. You didn't have to just leave Nashville and come back here. Why did you?"

"I thought ... you weren't coming back."

"Oh, darlin'."

She looked at him, saw the deep remorse written all over his face and the fury drained out of her. She took a deep breath, and gave a rueful smile.

His rigid shoulders relaxed, and he took a step toward her. She flinched, and he stopped abruptly, his eyes widening.

"My God, angel! What's the matter? Are you afraid of me?" He opened his arms, and she hesitated, then stepped into them, dropping her face on his shoulder, her tears soaking through his shirt. His arms tightened around her, his big hands caressing her back.

Relief coursed through her at the familiar feel of the heat of his strong body against her, his hands pressing gently against her back. Becky clung to the broad shoulders, her body absorbing the warm strength of him. She took several shuddering breaths, her tears abating.

"Put on your clothes, and let's get out of here." His voice rumbled against her.

She bobbed her head and pulled away. He looked at her with a small, crooked smile as she unzipped the tight cocktail dress, stepping out of it.

"Thank God I finally tracked you down," he said.

"Why did you go back to Nashville, Tripp?" she asked, fastening the garment on its hanger, totally unselfconscious in her skimpy bra and panties. "Aren't you still supposed to be out there someplace? The tour isn't supposed to be over yet, is it?"

"Nope. I'm off the tour. I left it. Something came up. Something important," he said, watching as she stuffed her stilettos into her tote bag and began to pull on her street clothes.

She looked at him questioningly, but he just smiled. She let it go; he would tell her when he was ready. She pulled on her coat.

He took her costumes off the rack, holding them over one arm. "You ready? Grab your tote, and let's get outta here. This place stinks. In more ways than one."

Becky followed him as he moved confidently toward the side door. "What are you driving?" he asked as they stepped out into the cold darkness at the side of the building.

"The red Pinto." Becky pointed.

He paused in mid step, raising his eyebrows. She ignored him and unlocked her little car. Tripp stepped around her and placed her dresses across the back seat. She pitched in the tote containing her makeup and shoes.

"We've got to have us a talk," Tripp said. "A pretty long one."

"Where's your car?" Becky asked nervously.

"It's parked here in the lot. Ain't you going to ask me how I found you?"

Becky frowned. "How *did* you find me?"

He looked at her, his face grim. "Can you imagine how I felt when I got back to our apartment, and you were gone? Just gone. Nobody had heard from you; you hadn't told a soul where you were going. The only consolation I had was that your suitcase and some of your clothes were gone. That's the only way I had to tell that you probably left willingly and hadn't been kidnapped or had an accident and was lying somewhere hurt or dead."

Her eyes rounded. "I'm sorry, Tripp!"

"You oughta be! I was nearly out of my mind."

"You came home early," she said. "You were supposed to still be off on the tour."

"Well, yeah, that part's true."

"I didn't have any way to call you. You guys were in and out of a town, and I didn't have any way to know where you were even going to be staying when you got somewhere."

"All that's true. That's the only reason that I don't want to wring your pretty, little neck. But you still scared me half to death when I couldn't find you."

"I told you I was sorry."

"Okay," he said, "but we're freezing our butts off standing out here in this parking lot in the middle of nowhere."

"You never did say how you found me."

"Well, I tried several times to call your sister in Phillips. I still had an old number for her where you had written it down in the front of our phone book. I never could get an answer there. But you used a credit card about a week ago to buy some gas, just outside Phillips. I'd put an alert on the Mastercard, and they called me."

"Oh, yeah!" said Becky. "I thought the card was maxed out, but then I thought maybe it had a little bit of room on it, so I tried it, and the charge went through."

"It's a damn good thing you did," he growled. "Otherwise, I might never have found you. When I flew into the Greensboro airport this evening, I tried your sister's number one final time. This time she was home, and I talked to her. She told me you were working for Jake again, and that's where I'd find you tonight. So, I rented a car and headed for Jake's. I had to talk to you before tomorrow."

"Tomorrow? What's tomorrow?" Becky's teeth were starting to chatter.

"Look! We're gonna go somewhere where it's warm and private. I told you that we've got a lot to talk about."

"Okay! Okay! What do you want to do?"

"I'm going to go get into my rental car. You follow me. I'm going to stop at the first decent-looking motel we pass, and we'll get a room." He glared at her. "When I pull out onto the highway, you'd better be right there behind me, Becky. Do you hear me?"

"Why don't we just go up to my sister's in Phillips? I'm staying at her house."

"We need to talk. Right now. Do you want to wake her up at this hour of the night? She knows I was coming to look for you at Jake's. So, she won't worry if you don't show up. You wanna go back there and get her out of bed?"

"No," she said meekly. "You go on. I'll follow you." She got into the Pinto and started the motor, watching him as he strode away through the rows of parked cars. She eased out and followed him. He got into a black, late-model rental car, his head turning toward her as he pulled out of his parking spot. She saw him watching her in his rearview mirror as he made his way toward the highway and signaled to turn. She followed him and gave him a little wave. The black rental car accelerated, and Becky followed him up the road.

A short time later, where the two-lane highway intersected with the interstate, Tripp signaled a turn toward the entrance of a brightly lighted chain motel beside the feeder road. Becky followed and pulled up beside his car as he stopped just outside the covered portico at the entrance. He walked to her car, and she rolled down the window.

"I'm going inside to register," he told her. "When I get a room, you follow me around to it."

"Okay," said Becky. She closed the window and waited as he went inside.

Minutes later, he came out and U-turned, pulling around to the back side of the motel. She followed and pulled into a parking spot beside him. He opened his trunk and pulled out a suitcase before walking up and opening the room door; he stepped inside, leaving it open. She got out of her car and followed him inside.

He set the suitcase down and turned to face her as she walked in. "Okay, Tripp," she said, "what's going on? Why did you quit the tour? And what's so gosh-darned important that you have to talk to me about it before tomorrow?"

He took two strides toward her and wrapped his arms around her. "Hello to you, too!" He grinned.

"Cut it out, Tripp! What's all this drama about?"

He looked at her and sighed, shaking his head as she glared at him. "Sit down. You're going to change your tune when you hear this. I guarantee you that."

There were an armchair and a little table with a straight-backed chair under the draped window. Becky sat down in the armchair. "I said I was sorry I worried you. Now tell me what's going on."

He pulled out the straight chair and, straddled it backward, looked at her over the slatted back. "Just the most important thing that's ever come up for your career," he said smugly.

She stared at him, her mind changing gears. "What?"

"I got a call while we were in Kansas City. Norm Alter from the recording studio was trying to reach me. You remember Norm?"

"Yeah. Front office. Handles the PR, stuff like that."

"Right. Well, he had a call from ABC Galaxy—that's an indie production company. ABC has the rights to a TV pilot for a series. Apparently, ABC showed it to the network, and they love it. As of right now, ABC has lined up most of the cast for this pilot. It's a drama about a country star and the people she works with, her family, and all that. The lead will sing at least one song in every episode, while all this drama takes place around her in the storyline. The president of ABC likes you. He insisted that you be contacted to see if you'd be interested in it."

Becky's eyes widened. "A TV show? They want *me* to audition for a TV show?"

Tripp's face split in a grin. "Yeah, they sure do."

"But … I've never acted. All I've ever done is sing."

"Doesn't matter! The president over at ABC has decided you're right for the part, and he wants to see you."

"Oh, my God," breathed Becky.

"So, I left the tour as soon as I heard the news, came home to tell you, and guess what? You were gone, and nobody knew where you were."

Becky stared at him, her mouth open, taking deep breaths.

"And, to make matters worse," Tripp said, "the guy's got to have someone signed by the first of the week *this week*. I need to get you to see him by tomorrow, or he's going to leave town and go find somebody else for the part." He spread out his hands. "Can you imagine what I've been going through? I was worried sick about you, didn't know where you were, and I had to find you and get you to see him by tomorrow!"

"Oh, my God, Tripp!"

"Is that all you can say? Do you have any idea how much this pays? More than we'll ever have a chance to make ever again. Why, the pilot alone pays more than you'd make in six months of appearances!"

"Do you really think I could do it?" Becky asked.

"Of course, you could! It's the chance of a lifetime. All I have to do is get you to a meeting with him by tomorrow afternoon so you can charm the heck out of him. He's already sold. All you have to do is show up!"

Becky's head was spinning. A laugh of pure joy bubbled out of her, and she felt a huge grin split her face. "Oh, my God, Tripp! Oh, my God!"

He jumped up, grabbed her, and pulled her to her feet, dancing her around the room. "See? What do you think of your manager now, angel? Huh? Huh?"

She danced with him, her head thrown back, feeling euphoric. Finally, they stopped, both of them breathless. "So, all I have to do is go meet with him, and I got it?" she asked. "He's going to make me the offer?"

"That's right! There's a flight out of Greensboro first thing in the morning. We can be there by noon. I'll call and set it up; he's waiting to hear from me. We can sleep here tonight and drop by your sister's early tomorrow to pick up your things. Then your dry spell will be over! Becky Barnes is back on the fast track again."

A sudden thought hit her. "Oh, no!" she exclaimed.

"Oh, no what?" Tripp looked at her.

Becky sank back down into her armchair. "I can't go. Not tomorrow."

He looked at her, incredulous. "Why not?" He grimaced. "If you're worried about appearing tomorrow night at Jake's club, forget it! This is huge! And it won't be the first time that one of Jake's performers has skipped out on him. He'll be mad as hell, but what can he do about it? He can announce that you had to go back to Nashville unexpectedly. You can call him tomorrow and tell him. No big deal."

"That's not it," said Becky. "I don't care about Jake."

"What then?" Tripp frowned at her.

She swallowed hard. "Benjie has a band recital tomorrow afternoon. I have to go."

"What? What band recital? Who's Benjie?"

"Benjie. My son. He invited me to come hear him play tomorrow. I have to be there."

"Your son?"

Becky took a deep breath. "Yes, Tripp. You remember I have a son. He was a baby when you and I … left. That's Benjie."

Tripp had a very odd expression. He continued to look at her. "So, how long have you been in contact with this son of yours—this Benjie? For all these years? Without telling me?"

"I wasn't! I never have been!" Becky cried defensively. "I know what you said when you took me to Nashville. You told me I had to cut all ties with everybody back here. But you know that I've never said anything about him. I've never even mentioned his name to you. I didn't complain about leaving him behind ... Tripp, I didn't!"

He stared at her. "Oh, Becky!" he said in a low voice.

She twisted her hands together, and she felt her face screw up, trying to hold back the hot tears she felt forming. "I never said anything to you ... I didn't!"

He closed his eyes, and something like a shudder ran through his body. She stared at him as he sat silently, eyes closed, his lips pressed together. Finally, he took a deep, shuddering breath and opened his eyes. "Becky," he said quietly, "what are you saying to me?"

She just looked back at him without speaking, but she felt her lips quiver.

He raised both hands and rubbed his face. His head went backward, and he sighed deeply. Looking at her again, he said, "Becky, please tell me what's going through that head of yours."

"What do you mean?" she asked, her voice quavering in spite of herself.

"Why did you leave Nashville and come back here to North Carolina?" he asked. "And why didn't you tell me you were coming? Was it about this Benjie? Is that what this is about?"

Her mouth twisted, but she didn't speak; she simply shook her head.

"Were you afraid to say something to me?" His voice was soft.

Becky shook her head again. "You told me never to complain, not to look back," she said woodenly. "I never have."

"Oh, Becky! After all our years together ... after everything we've been through, did you really think you couldn't tell me you wanted to come here?"

She dropped her head. "Yes."

"Oh, my God, Becky! You know how much I love you. What I said to you ..." He closed his eyes again. He took a deep breath and looked at her again. "Becky, those were the words of a brash young man who was scared to death that he would lose the best thing he'd ever found!"

"Really?"

"Oh, yes! Really."

Becky sighed.

Tripp walked over to her and enclosed her loosely in his long arms. "Tell me about it, honey. Why did you come back here after all these years? Please tell me."

She rested her bowed head against his shoulder. "I didn't have anything much to do after you left," she said. "I got to thinking … and I couldn't get Benjie out of my mind."

"Benjie … you and Quinn's little boy."

"Uh-huh. I was so lonesome, Tripp. I kept wondering how he was … how he'd turned out. I just wanted to see him, to talk to him."

"Okay."

She raised her head to look at him out of her tear-streaked face. "There was just a tiny, little bit of money left in our account. I drew it out and bought me a bus ticket."

Tripp sighed. "You came here on the bus."

She nodded. "It wasn't too bad."

He grimaced. "So, did you get to talk to Benjie like you wanted to? Obviously, you've seen him."

She smiled through her tears. "Sort of! It sure wasn't easy. Quinn didn't want me anywhere near him. He's still mad at me for leaving him all those years ago."

Tripp snorted. "Sure can't blame him for that!"

"I got to talk to Benjie for a few minutes one time." Her eyes lit up. "He told me he's playing drums in a little band tomorrow afternoon, and he invited me to come hear him play."

"That's good, honey, that's good," Tripp told her soothingly.

"But Benjie will understand that you can't be there tomorrow. Becky, did you even hear what I told you? We've got to get you to that meeting. This is the break that you've been waiting for. I thought you'd be out of your mind when you heard about it!"

"I am, Tripp! I really am. You did a wonderful job lining this up for me. This is better than anything I ever even dreamed of happening. It scares me to death. It's so good! But Benjie—"

"Benjie will understand."

"He's fourteen years old. Do you really think so?"

"Yes, I do," Tripp replied firmly.

She bit her lip. "I really, really do want to go after this," she murmured.

"Of course, you do!" Tripp gave her a little shake. "It's the chance of a lifetime!"

"The starring role in an ongoing TV series," Becky said softly, her lips curving into an unconscious smile.

"It was made for you," he said. "You get to sing in every episode in front of an audience of millions. We could introduce a new song on the show, and I'll bet it'd go platinum!"

"Oh, Tripp!"

"Yeah!" he said, excitement in his voice. "I told you. It's the chance of a lifetime!"

"Are you sure, Tripp? Are you sure that he wants *me* for the part?"

"One hundred percent positive."

Becky's eyes got a faraway look in them, and she smiled broadly. "And the money! I'd be making some real money."

"You bet your life you'd be making real money! This is it, baby! This is what we've always dreamed of happening."

"I could fly Benjie out to Nashville to visit. He could come and see me on the set!"

Tripp nodded. "Yeah, you sure could."

Her eyes gleamed. "All right! Oh, Tripp, this is so wonderful!"

His arms tightened around her. "Now you're talking, baby! Now, how about a big ol' welcome home kiss for ol' Tripp, here?" He lowered his mouth to hers.

Becky felt her body begin to respond as his mouth moved over hers hungrily. He urged her backward onto the bed, his hands moving possessively over her. But a small sliver of doubt tempered her excitement.

Am I making another huge mistake? she wondered. *Will Benjie really understand? Will I be deserting him again?*

Chapter Fourteen

The sound of a telephone, loud and piercing, began to penetrate Becky's consciousness. She felt movement beside her in the warm bed. Her body, groggy and replete after her recent lovemaking, was sinking back down into oblivion when a hand on her shoulder shook her none too gently.

"C'mon, honey, we gotta get up." She heard Tripp's gravelly voice next to her ear. She groaned.

"No-ooo," she grumbled again as he continued to shake her.

"C'mon, you can take a nap on the plane. We gotta go," he insisted.

"Wha' time is it?" Her eyelids felt like they were glued shut.

"Four thirty." He sounded much too cheerful. "I left a wake-up call. Get up, darlin'! We gotta get you to your sister's so you can pack. Then we've got to drive all the way back over to the Greensboro airport. We've got a plane to catch."

"Five more minutes," she mumbled, trying to grab the covers.

"Up!" he said, and she felt the covers leave her naked body, the cool air in the room hitting her skin like a deluge of cold water.

"We only slept for an hour." She rose to a sitting position.

"I know. But we've got a lot of driving to do—over to Phillips, then back to the airport."

"I'll look like shit for our meeting today."

"You could never do that," he told her. "Besides, like I said, you can sleep on the plane. C'mon on now—we've got to get on the road."

Reluctantly, she swung her feet to the floor and began searching for her discarded clothing through her half-open eyes.

After they left, Tripp went through the drive-through of a McDonald's next to the motel, and the big, hot cup of coffee made her feel nearly half alive as they took off in their separate cars up the interstate toward Phillips.

Clara's car was still in the driveway when they reached the house. She was in the kitchen, and the coffeepot was sending off fragrant fumes as they both walked in the side door.

"Tripp, this is my sister, Clara," Becky said. "I don't believe the two of you have ever met."

Clara raised her eyebrows and gave him a once-over as he approached her and wrapped his long arms around her.

"It's a real pleasure, Clara," he rumbled, grinning at Becky over Clara's shoulder. "We've talked on the phone, but it's nice to see you in person."

"What's going on, Becky?" Clara asked her sharply as she disengaged.

"Tripp's got a really good deal lined up for me," Becky told her. "The only problem is, it has to be signed off on today. We have to get to Nashville before this afternoon for a meeting, or I won't get it."

"Is that so?" said Clara. She gave Becky a hard look. "What about your promise to Benjie? You're supposed to go hear him play today."

"This is a really huge deal," Becky's voice was pleading. "It means more money than I ever made in my life. It's a shot at my having the lead on a TV show. I can't begin to tell you how big this is."

Clara just looked at her silently.

"Please, Clara. You can explain it to Benjie for me. You can make him understand," said Becky.

"There'll be other times when she can see Benjie play," Tripp said, finding a mug and pouring himself a cup of Clara's coffee.

"He will understand. Won't he Clara?" said Becky.

Clara sighed. "I hope you know what you're doing," she said. "I've got to get to the diner. I'm going to be late."

"You better get packed," said Tripp to Becky. "We've got to hurry. Our flight leaves at nine."

Becky grabbed Clara's hands in hers. "Please, Clara. You'll let him know what happened, won't you? Please do me a favor and tell him."

Clara sighed again. "All right. I'll tell him."

Becky dropped her sister's hands and rushed out of the room.

"Do you know what she's been trying to do here?" Clara asked Tripp.

"I think so," he said. "She wanted to get to know her son."

"That's right. I don't think this is the way to do it, breaking her promise to him this way."

"She can make it up to him later."

"You sure about that?" asked Clara.

"Clara, this deal is huge. It's worth a lot of money. Becky can't afford to miss out on it."

"I can understand that," said Clara. "But I wonder if Benjie will."

Tripp didn't answer.

In the bedroom, Becky threw her clothes into the old suitcase, untidily emptying drawers into it. She snapped it shut and stopped dead still as an idea hit her.

"Have you got a piece of paper, a pen, and an envelope?" she asked, running back out into the kitchen.

"In the drawer of the hall table," said Clara. "What do you need that for?"

Becky didn't reply. She got what she needed and ran back into the bedroom. Using her suitcase as a desktop, she wrote "For Benjie" in big letters on the envelope. Closing her eyes in thought for a moment, she wrote a note on the blank piece of paper.

> Dear Benjie,
>
> I'm so sorry that I had to leave town and miss hearing you play. I'll hear you some other time. I promise. I'm going back to Nashville to work, and I won't need my car anymore, so I want you to have it. Here's the keys, and the title is in the glove box. I never did get around to putting it in my name, so you just put it in yours.
>
> Love, Becky Barnes (your birth mom)

She wrapped the car keys inside the note and stuck the note inside the envelope. She licked the envelope, pressing it sealed over the bulky contents.

"You ready?" asked Tripp as she came back into the kitchen.

"Yes. Will you get my suitcase?"

He walked past her to get it.

The two sisters looked at each other for a long moment. Becky handed Clara the fat envelope. "Give that to Benjie for me, will you?" she asked.

Clara took it and looked at it with a frown. "All right."

Becky threw her arms around her sister. "I'm going to miss you, sis!"

Clara hugged her back. "I'm going to miss you, too, Beck. You take care of yourself."

Tripp walked past them, carrying the suitcase. "We need to hurry, hon," he said. "We don't want to miss our flight."

"You sure you know what you're doing?" asked Clara.

"No!" admitted Becky. "Listen, do you think you could come out to Nashville to visit me? If this works out, I can buy you an airline ticket so you can come, and you can stay with me and Tripp. I'd pay all your expenses."

Clara looked at her, and a slow smile lifted her lips. "I guess I could do that," she said. "I ain't had a vacation since … well, since never, I guess."

"Becky!" called Tripp.

"I'm giving Benjie my car," said Becky. "That's what's in the envelope—the keys to it."

Clara's smile grew. "That should be interesting," she said.

"I really do have to go," said Becky. Her face almost crumpled. "Do you think it will be all right?"

Clara put her arms around her sister. "Yeah. I think it will." She released her. "But you'll need to come back pretty soon."

"I will," promised Becky. She turned and ran out to where Tripp was waiting in his rental car, the motor running.

Clara watched as they drove away. She pulled the door closed behind her and started toward her car to drive to work.

Chapter Fifteen

"Cut!" said the director. "All right, people. That's it. That's a wrap. See you on Monday."

The actor she was sharing an embrace with let go of her, and Becky stood up as conversations broke out all around them on the set. She looked across, just beyond the circle of cameras, and a big smile broke across her face. She ran across to two people standing there and threw her arms around her sister.

"Clara! You made it! You're really here," she cried happily.

Tripp was grinning inanely. "Yeah, I got her here from the airport just in time for her to see you shoot that last scene. What did you think, Clara?"

"It sure didn't look anything like it does when I watch it on TV," said Clara. "All those people crowded up around you and those cameras aimed at you from all angles, just inches from your face. I don't know how you remember what you need to say."

Becky laughed. "Sure takes all the romance out of it, doesn't it? How was your flight?"

"Good, I guess, since it was the first time in my life I ever flew, and I don't have nothing to compare it to."

"Come on, let me get back to my dressing room, get out of these clothes, and get my makeup off. Then Tripp and I are going to show you around Nashville, if you're not too tired, and then we're taking you out to dinner." Becky hugged her sister again. "I'm so glad that you could come."

"Me, too," said Clara, her head swiveling back and forth as people moved purposefully around them; she was taking it all in. "I'm not tired at all."

Half an hour later, they were in Tripp's car, and he was driving them around the city, pointing out landmarks to Clara. "That's the Grand Ole Opry building there on the right," he said.

"Oh, my," said Clara. "Do you think I could see inside it while I'm here?"

"Oh, yeah. They have tours of the building almost every day. Maybe we could even get tickets to a show while you're here."

"And this is where you live," said Clara in an awed voice. "I'll bet you see some of the real big stars all the time."

"Every once in a while," replied Becky, amused. "Do you want to get something to eat, or do you want to go to our apartment first?"

"Whichever is more convenient for you," replied Clara. "I'm fine."

"Let's get something to eat then," said Tripp. "I could go for an early dinner tonight. Then you can rest some tonight, angel. You're not on the schedule, so we can all play tourist tomorrow."

"Sounds good to me," said Becky. She switched on the car radio to a country station.

Tripp pulled the car to the front entrance of a restaurant. Seconds later, valets were opening the doors on each side of the vehicle. Becky got out and stood aside as the valet offered a hand for Clara, assisting her out of the back seat. The door was closed, and the valet on the driver's side climbed in, and the car rolled away. The second valet held the restaurant door wide, and the three of them entered.

The maître d' came hurrying to meet them, smiling. "Mr. Thomas! Miss Barnes!" he said. "So happy to see you today."

"A table for three, please, Charles," said Tripp.

"Certainly! Right this way please." They were led into the quiet, dimly lit restaurant and to a table near the wall. Instantly, a waiter was there; Charles and the waiter pulled back their chairs and seated Becky and Clara.

Becky was watching her sister as she saw Clara covertly looking around the room, taking in the elegant fixtures and the linen-draped tables. She saw her sister start as the waiter whisked her linen napkin from the tabletop and across her lap. He handed them the tall, leather-bound menus, while a busboy appeared tableside and was pouring ice water into the stemmed glasses at their places.

"Give us a moment or two, please," said Tripp, taking his menu.

"Certainly, Mr. Thomas," said the waiter, backing away with a little bow.

They studied the menus. "What looks good to you, ladies?" Tripp asked.

Becky sighed. "I guess I need to just eat the salad," she said. "I can't afford to put on a single ounce, or it will show up on camera. What do you want, Clara? Pick out anything you want."

Clara closed her menu and looked over the table at them. "I have no idea what most of this stuff even is," she admitted, her forehead furrowed. "What are you ordering?"

"I'm going to have the prime rib," said Tripp. "And a nice glass of wine with it. Of course, Becky will just have her water. She doesn't drink anymore. What do you want tonight, angel?"

Becky made a face. "Just a salad. Dry."

Clara narrowed her eyes. "So, nothing has changed, huh, Beck? When you're working for Jake and got no money, you're eating a bowl of lettuce. Now you're the star of a TV show, and you're still eating a bowl of lettuce."

Becky's face crinkled into a warm laugh. "I guess you're right. The only thing that's changed is the cost of my bowl of lettuce."

"And the surroundings," added Tripp.

"Why don't we order her the beef medallions with burgundy sauce," said Becky. "I think she'll like that."

"What's that?" asked Clara suspiciously.

"It's three or four little, round pieces of very tender beef with a wonderful-tasting sauce poured over the top of it," explained Becky.

"All right."

"Maybe I'll steal one of your medallions," said Becky. "It's one of my favorite things they make here."

Clara's smile grew more relaxed. "Deal," she said.

They ordered and were enjoying their meal when Clara froze and stared across the room, her water glass halfway to her lips. Her hand began shaking.

"What is it?" Becky asked her in a loud whisper. "Clara, what's wrong?"

Clara carefully lowered her glass to the table, her gaze fixed across the room. "Over there," she whispered back. "Who is that, sitting over there? Is that who I think it is?"

"I can't look," said Becky. "My back is toward the room. Tripp, who is it?"

Tripp pretended to drop his napkin, looking to his right as he retrieved it. "Oh," he said quietly. "That's Reba McEntire sitting over there with her husband, Narvel Blackstock."

"I thought so!" said Clara. "I thought that's who it was. Oh, my God! Nobody will believe this when I tell them I ate in the same restaurant with Reba!"

Becky laughed aloud. "Now I've finally arrived!" She chortled. "I've finally done something to impress my sister!"

Tripp chuckled. He raised his wineglass. "Welcome to Nashville, Clara," he said.

When they finished their meal, Tripp drove them a short distance away from the main part of town and into a parking garage beside an apartment building.

"So, this is where you live?" Clara asked as they rode up the elevator.

"Yep," said Becky. "We moved here after I got the TV show."

Tripp set Clara's suitcase down as they stepped out of the elevator into a brightly lit, little foyer with two doorways facing the elevator. He walked over to the one on the left and unlocked the oversized white door. A glass table stood against the wall between the two doors, a huge arrangement of fresh flowers sitting on it, filling the area with fragrance.

Tripp picked up the suitcase and stepped inside. He flicked on lights as he entered, holding the door wide so the two women could follow him.

"Oh, wow!" exclaimed Clara, looking around the living room as she entered it. The room looked very modern with its white couch and chairs, flanked by the glass and chrome end tables and coffee table. A large rug covered most of the hardwood floor, and there was a white brick fireplace at the far side of the room, between two large floor-to-ceiling windows. Except for four guitars resting on racks to one side of the room, no personal touches were evident. An abstract painting in reds and yellows provided almost the only color in the room. Clara followed them across the room, past a stainless steel and chrome kitchen area on the right, which looked totally unused, to a doorway at the head of a short hallway.

"This is your room," Becky said, pushing the door open. "Our bedroom is down at the end of the hall. The bathroom next to this room is all yours."

The room was small but very pretty. It was carpeted in beige, and the bed was covered with a yellow and white spread, colors echoed in the yellow- and white-striped drapes over a small window. A single armchair, upholstered in solid yellow with white pillows, sat beside the window, and a bedside table held a lamp with a white shade.

"There's towels and soap and everything you might need in the bathroom next door," said Becky as Tripp brought in her suitcase and left it on the floor in front of the closet door. "If you need anything I didn't think of, just tell me. I'm going to go down to my room, take a bath, and put on something comfy. Do you want to bathe and change after your trip, Clara?"

"I think I will," said Clara.

"Okay." Becky smiled at her. "Come on out to the living room when you finish. We'll have something to drink and catch up."

Clara took the time to put away the clothes she had packed in her suitcase, neatly hanging them in the empty closet using the ample supply of hangers she found there and putting her undergarments in the drawers of a built-in dresser in the closet. She took a pair of slacks and a roomy top, along with a change of lingerie into the bathroom with her. She placed them on top of the counter there, admiring the sparkling-clean newness of the room. It looked as though she were the first person ever to use it. She disrobed and allowed herself the luxury of a long, hot shower, toweling herself dry afterward with one of the thickest, fluffiest towels she'd ever seen.

After she dressed and walked into the living room, she saw that her sister was already there, half reclining on the white couch and dressed in a set of dark green velour lounge pants and top, her feet bare.

"Hey!" said Becky as Clara hesitated in the area beside the kitchen. "Come on in here. Grab yourself a soda. See that little fridge there at the end of the bar beside you? Help yourself."

Clara looked where Becky was pointing and opened the tiny refrigerator, finding it stocked with a selection of canned drinks. She pulled out a can of Coke and joined Becky.

Becky pulled up her legs and motioned for her to sit beside her on the sofa.

"Where's Tripp?" Clara asked as she sat down.

"Oh, he went out. He's meeting somebody to talk over some of the details for next week's script or something. He really just wanted to give us some time alone together tonight."

Clara swiveled her head around, taking a good look at her surroundings. "This is pretty," she said.

Becky made a face. "We like it," she said. "It's new and uncluttered."

Clara popped her drink can and took a sip of the cold liquid.

"It sure beats the rattrap we were living in before," Becky added softly.

"It's beautiful," Clara told her.

Becky drew her knees up to her chin and circled her legs with her arms as she sat sidewise on the sofa, facing her sister. "So, tell me what's going on in Phillips," she said.

"Not much," said Clara. She smiled ruefully. "In other words, everything's just like it always is."

"How's Benjie?"

Clara reached out and put her hand on Becky's knee. "Benjie's fine. He's as busy as a boy can possibly be—into every activity you can imagine."

"What happened when I left?" Becky's voice was just louder than a whisper. "Tell me again. I want to hear it straight from you in person. Did he understand why I had to go? Why I had to miss his program that day?"

"Yes, I think he did," Clara reassured her for what must have been the tenth time. "I had Donna bring him into the diner that same day that you left, and I told him myself. He understood."

Tears glittered in Becky's eyes. "What about the car?" she asked. "Did he like it that I left him my car for a present?"

Clara's lips curved into a satisfied smile. "Oh, yeah! I handed him that envelope you left him myself! I wanted to make absolutely sure he knew about the car and who it came from. I wish you could have seen his face when he read the note, and I explained to him that it was a little, red Pinto and that it was being given to him by you."

"What did his parents say?" Becky asked eagerly.

Clara chuckled. "You should have seen Donna's face. She didn't know what to say. But Benjie was so happy, bouncing up and down, and wanting to know when he could come and get his car." Clara laughed again. "I sure wish I could have been a fly on the wall when they told Quinn!"

"What happened after that?" asked Becky.

"Oh, a week or so afterward, Donna called me and wanted to know when they could come and get Benjie's car. I told her anytime they wanted to. So, one day after work, all of them came by the house, and Quinn drove it home—with Benjie and little Sammy riding in it with him! Donna and Amy Lynne followed them home in their car."

"I'd give a lot to have seen that," said Becky. "I wonder what they did with it."

"Well, Benjie told me it was in their garage, waiting for him to get to be sixteen years old so he could drive it."

Becky smiled.

"That reminds me," said Clara. "I brought you something." She got up and went back to her bedroom. Becky watched as she came back in and sat back down on the sofa.

"Here." Clara handed her a small photo. "That's Benjie's school picture for this year. He told me to bring it to you."

Becky stared down at the photo and burst into tears.

Clara grabbed her in her arms, hugging her tight. "I'm sorry, Becky! I thought you'd be happy to get this."

"I am! Oh, God, Clara, you have no idea," sobbed Becky. She looked at the photo and cried harder. "Do you know that this is the only picture I've ever had of my boy? The only one!"

"I'd never thought about it," said Clara, holding her. "I had no idea."

"Oh, Clara, this is the best present I've ever had," said Becky, her head on Clara's shoulder, her tears wetting through Clara's blouse. "Thank you! Thank you so much."

"Hey, girls!" Tripp's voice boomed through the room a couple of hours later as he came through the front door. "Have you had a good visit?"

"We have," Becky responded cheerily.

"Are you about caught up with your gossip? Going to be ready to go sightseeing tomorrow?"

"Yes," said Clara, smiling at him. "We sure are."

*C*hapter Sixteen

On Sunday evening, they took showers and met back in Becky's living room after a long, second day of sightseeing.

Tripp leaned down and gave Becky a light kiss on her lips as she sat with her legs curled up under her on the sofa. "I'm going back to our room and work on that song I've been struggling with, try to get the words to come out right. I'll leave you girls to talk. Becky, don't you stay up too late—you know you've got to be there early in the morning. Clara, you can sleep in a little bit late. I'll be here to take you to breakfast and on back to the airport for your flight out in the morning. I'm real glad you could come visit us. It's meant a whole lot to Becky, and I enjoyed seeing you, too."

"I had fun," Clara told him. "Thank you so much for driving us around to all those places. I really enjoyed seeing the Belle Meade Plantation—and the Country Music Hall of Fame and all the places you took me during the last two days. I really had a good time."

Tripp put his arm around her and gave her a hug. "It was my pleasure, Clara. You girls enjoy visiting now. I'll see you in the morning."

"He's a real nice man," Clara told Becky after he disappeared from the room. "You're real lucky."

"I know it," said Becky with a smile.

"Seems like you two are really happy," Clara said wistfully.

Becky nodded.

Clara gave a little laugh and looked around the room. "This sure is a far cry from Phillips."

Becky raised her eyebrow. "Yep. It sure is. But I'm not taking it for granted, not for a single second. I know how easy it is for things to change in this business. We could be back to me without a job and living in a little two-room rattrap of an apartment in the blink of an eye."

"You're saving some of the money you're making, aren't you?" Clara asked her quickly. "I mean … I don't intend to pry into your business, but …"

"Oh, yeah!" Becky assured her, waving a hand in the air. "You'd better believe it. I don't ever again want to have to live off ramen noodles and worry if I'll be out in the street because I can't pay the rent."

Clara took a deep breath of relief. "That's good to know," she said.

"We got us a financial adviser right after I got my first check, and I'm socking money away for the future."

"Good," said Clara.

"That song … the one we finally heard play on the radio this afternoon," Becky began.

"Oh, yeah! 'Love Me Yesterday'—your new song," said Clara.

Becky nodded happily. "Uh-huh. 'Love Me Yesterday'—it's starting to take off a little. We're hoping it will become a hit."

"I'm going to call in to the radio station when I get home and ask them to play it," said Clara.

"Atta girl! That's what I need to happen all over the place. That's what will give it a boost. Then maybe I'll have me a new hit." Becky leaned back, closed her eyes, and sang softly, "'Today is almost over … tomorrow you'll be gone … so turn back the time and love me yesterday.'"

"It's a real pretty song," said Clara.

"We introduced it on the TV show," said Becky. "We were hoping that would give it a big boost, being heard all over the United States when the show aired."

"That's where I first heard it," said Clara. "When you sang it on your show."

"You watch my show?" asked Becky happily.

"Of course, I do, silly."

They sat in companionable silence for a moment. "You know what, Clara?" Becky said softly. "I used to think you were jealous of me."

Clara looked sharply at her. "Jealous? Why would I be jealous of you?"

"Well," Becky said, looking uncomfortable, "because … because I had Quinn and then Tripp … and it seemed like you just never had anybody."

"What makes you say that?" asked Clara with a little smile.

"Clara Smith!" Becky sat up. "Are you trying to tell me that you had somebody? Did you have a secret lover nobody knows about?"

A slow flush spread over Clara's face.

"You did!" Becky squealed. "I can see it written all over your face. You have to tell me about it now!"

"But I didn't … not really," murmured Clara.

"You were always so quiet! I didn't know a thing about it. Who was he?"

Clara shook her head with a little smile. "It was nothing. Really."

"What happened? Tell me, Clara!" cried Becky eagerly.

"Nothing. Nothing really happened," said Clara, averting her head.

"Why not?"

"Because! He had his obligations, his duties. And I had to take care of Mama."

Becky leaned forward and took both of Clara's hands in hers. "Tell me about it, Clara, please," she said softly.

"There's nothing to tell. Really. Nothing happened."

"But you fell in love," Becky persisted. "Didn't you?"

Clara nodded, her eyes looking down.

"Oh, sis! Please tell me. What happened? When was this? I won't tell a soul, I promise. Was he married or something?"

"No. That wasn't it."

Becky slipped an arm around Clara's shoulders. "Please tell me."

Clara sighed. "It was after you left—after you and Tripp run off together."

"Okay. Go on."

"This was maybe the summer after you left," Clara said in a soft, dreamy voice, her eyes seemingly focused on another place. "There was going to be this big church revival. All three of the Baptist churches in the area joined together, and they set up this big, old tent filled with folding chairs down beside Lone Hickory Road in a big pasture. I think it was on the Willis Adams farm. They set up tables outside the tent, and everybody was supposed to bring a dish of food so we could have dinner on the ground before the meeting. And they had some missionaries who were coming in to lead the preaching.

"One of the missionaries was a well-known pastor from here in the US, but two of the missionaries were black men who had come all the way from South Africa, traveling all around the country before they went back home. So, our little white church in Phillips, the one over in Madiera, and the black church, Mission Hill Baptist, just outside Phillips (the one that Al's cook, Miss Carrie, goes to), all three of them got together to have this big revival together.

"We didn't know anything about it until the Friday night of that week. Mama heard about it from some of the neighbors and decided she wanted to go. She didn't get out much by then, and it was so rare that she ever wanted to go anywhere, so I got her into the car after I got home from work, and we went over there."

"What happened?" asked Becky.

Clara shrugged. "Not too much. I got Mama to sit down, fixed a plate of food for her, and we talked to some folks while we ate. I took her on into the tent so she could get a good seat down close to the front. Reverend Parks, who was our pastor, came over and said a few words to Mama and he had me walk up toward the front with him so he could introduce me to that preacher I told you was so well known, the one who was heading up the revival." Clara laughed. "I can't even tell you what his name was right now. I guess he didn't make a very big impression on me.

"Anyway, while we was standing there, the two visiting missionaries, the ones from South Africa, walked up. Reverend Parks introduced me to the older one; he seemed like a real nice man. He shook my hand and told me he was glad to meet me. Then I turned toward the other one, and oh, Becky, I almost died on the spot! I looked up into a pair of the softest, kindest, most gentle brown eyes I'd ever seen in my whole life. They were like lakes of deep, soothing water I felt like I could just sink down into and never come up!" Clara gave a little laugh. "You probably think I'm crazy to say that."

Becky squeezed her hand. "No, I don't," she said. "What happened then?"

Clara laughed self-consciously. "Oh, I don't know! Reverend Parks introduced him to me, said his name was Kary Omari, and he reached out and took hold of my hand." Clara glanced down at her small, worn hand with its slender fingers. "His big, warm fingers just closed over mine like a glove. Reverend Parks was telling him what a good woman I was, that I was taking care of my invalid mother, blah-blah-blah. All I knew was that he was holding onto my hand and looking down at me with this gentle, little smile. It sounds silly, but something passed between us like a bolt of electricity."

"It doesn't sound silly to me at all," said Becky. "Then what did you do?"

Clara shrugged. "I went and sat down in the chair beside Mama. All three of the preachers sat down on some chairs up behind the podium, and they took turns. All three of them got up and gave a sermon. Every time I looked up there, to where he was sitting, he was staring straight at me." She sighed. "This went on and on, and we didn't get home until late; it was way past the time we usually went to bed. And, of course, I had to get up real early next morning and go to work at the diner, like always." Clara smiled a little smile. "Miss Carrie was already there, mixing up the dough for the biscuits. She'd seen us there the night before, and she just couldn't talk enough about how wonderful the service had been last night. She just went on and on about it. We talked about it the whole time we worked that day."

"So, Miss Carrie was there. Were there many of the black folks from Missionary Hill there?"

"Oh, yes! I'd say they made up about maybe a quarter of the folks that was there, all scattered through the crowd, all of us sitting there together in those rows of folding chairs. They had put up big, old temporary lights on high posts all around the inside edges of the tent, and those bright lights sure made it hot in there, and there we were in our Sunday clothes, sweating on those hard chairs. But everybody was listening, all caught up in the singing and the preaching. Everybody was having a good time." Clara had a distant look on her face, lost in her memory.

"So, what happened then?" asked Becky. "I guess you all went back that last night, didn't you?"

"Well, I was ready to, but when I got home from work, Mama was all cross and grumpy. She said she was tired out from the night before and didn't want to go back again." Clara looked at Becky, her eyes shining. "But for once, I told her that I was going, whether she did or not. I changed out of my uniform, fed her, and got her settled in for the night. Then I got in the car, and I drove myself over there. I left Mama by herself at home. I took a seat on the aisle, close to the back of the tent. The other missionary, the older man, talked first. Then Kary got up and walked over to speak.

"Oh, Becky, he was such a beautiful man! His skin was real dark, and it shone like it was polished, and he had the prettiest white teeth that just flashed when he smiled. He had on a suit and a shirt and tie, and it looked like it was tailor-made for him. When he spoke, he didn't jump around and make his voice rise and fall, yelling and waving his arms, like some of them revival preachers do. He stood there with his hands resting on the podium, and his voice just poured out over us like honey, talking about God's love, and how we could make a difference in the world through being kind and good to one another, taking care of each other. Everyone just sat and didn't make a sound. They just listened to him speak, with that wonderful accent of his making his words sound like music. After he finished and sat down, that famous preacher who was with them got up and began to speak. That's when I looked up there, and Kary caught my eye. He made a little sideways motion with his head to me and looked hard at me. He got up and slipped away through where the pieces of the tent came together behind where they were sitting up front behind the altar."

"What did you do?" asked Becky, totally caught up in her sister's story.

Clara smiled. "I got up, and I slipped out the back entrance of the tent. I walked up toward the front end of the tent until I saw him standing there, waiting for me. When I got up there, even with him, he didn't say a word. He just took hold of my hand, and we walked off across the field, out back past the rows of parked cars. We stopped when we got to the far edge of the field." Clara laughed. "It was just like in a movie. It wasn't full dark. There was maybe a half-moon in the sky. He turned around to face me, and the only thing I could think of to say was, 'How in the world did you get a name like Kary?'"

"What did he say?" breathed Becky.

"He just laughed at me with that beautiful smile of his. He told me that the reason people called him Kary was that they couldn't say his real name right. He said his real name was Dakari, which means 'happiness' in his language, and his last name is Omari, which means 'God the Highest.' He told me that he was so happy that I came back tonight and that he'd been thinking about me all day long and wondering if I would. He looked down at me and told me that he saw a wonderful light shining inside me, like a living flame. He just stared down into my eyes, like he'd never stop looking." Clara's voice trembled as she spoke.

"Did he kiss you?" asked Becky softly.

"No." Clara laughed, a shaky little sound in the room. "I kissed *him*! I reached up with both my hands and put them on the back of his head and pulled his head down, and I kissed him." She closed her eyes, remembering how hard her heart was beating at her boldness, recalling the softness of his lips as they met hers and how their kiss had deepened. It had done so with such aching tenderness and yearning that at last, when they pulled apart, both of them were trembling.

"'If we could combine this fire within us,' he had whispered, 'the whole world would light up like day. But much as we want it, you know that this can never be.'" Clara sat silently, staring off into space, remembering everything—the hot, little breeze that had surrounded them, the muted sounds of the revival meeting coming from the tent in the distance, right down to the tiny bead of sweat that ran down his neck.

"Clara!" Becky was saying. "Talk to me! You can't just leave it hanging like this. Tell me what happened then?"

"We talked for a little while," Clara told her. "We stood there and just talked. Finally, he said that we had to go back, or we would be missed, and that's what we did. He slipped back inside the tent. But my legs were trembling so bad I just couldn't go back in. I got into my car and drove home. I never saw him again."

"Oh, Clara! That's awful!" cried Becky.

"It wouldn't have worked out—we both knew that!" said Clara. "I had my obligations, and he had his. I had to take care of Mama, and they would have thrown him out of the church if they knew we'd even touched. He was black, and I was white! He told me that they had a wife picked out for him to marry when he got back home. She was a good woman, he told me, and it was his duty to marry her and have children with her. He was going to establish a church there and help the people of his community where so much needed to be done. What we felt for each other was impossible."

Clara gave a little laugh, but her eyes glittered with unshed tears. "If Mama was scandalized when you ran off with Tripp and left Quinn and Benjie, can you imagine what she would have said if I had brought home a black man? Can you imagine the talk all over town? And he couldn't have stayed here—the church would have disowned him, and he wouldn't have had a job, and he would have had to go back to South Africa in disgrace. And I couldn't have left here and gone there either. Could you imagine me in South Africa? He wouldn't have had a job, and neither would I. No. We did the only thing we could have done. We walked away and kept on going, putting one foot in front of the other."

"Oh, my God, Clara!"

"Are you upset with me?" asked Clara in a small voice.

"Upset? No! I think that's … beautiful. Oh, Clara!"

They sat in silence for a few minutes.

"I guess I'm having a hard time picturing you married to a black man with two or three little, kinky-headed, dark-skinned kids hanging onto your skirt and calling you 'Mama,'" commented Becky, smiling. "We-ell, maybe I can see it, at that."

Clara smiled. "But they would have had their father's beautiful, gentle brown eyes," she said. "They would have been beautiful."

"Yes, they would have," said Becky, and the two of them embraced.

"God, Clara," said Becky after she released her sister, and several more minutes had passed. "Is that the only man you've ever wanted?"

"I guess so," Clara said. "Nobody else looked good to me when I held him up against the picture I have of Kary in my mind."

"Maybe, someday …" Becky started to say.

"No, I don't think so," said Clara firmly.

The two sisters sat silently for a time, each lost in her own thoughts.

"Thank you for coming to visit me," said Becky at last. "And thank you for sharing that story with me. It means a lot to me that you did."

"I didn't think I'd ever tell anybody," Clara confessed. "I guess I'm glad I told you, though."

"We're sisters," said Becky. "That's what sisters do."

Chapter Seventeen

Early on the Friday morning after Clara got back home from her visit, she had just finished delivering the breakfast plates to her usual table of six to eight seniors. They met every morning at the diner for a hearty meal, lingering over coffee for at least an hour while they discussed politics, world affairs, and their various health issues.

The door to the diner creaked open, and Quinn Cavanaugh strode in, his face like a thundercloud. He headed straight toward Clara.

"Where is he?" he demanded as he stopped two feet away, towering over her. "Where's my boy?"

"What are you talking about, Quinn?" asked Clara. All conversation at the nearby table of seniors stopped and all eyes turned toward them.

Quinn glowered at her. "Benjie's missing. Do you know where he is?"

Clara's knees turned to water. "No!" She gasped. "What are you talking about? What do you mean, Benjie's missing?"

He grasped her arm. "Are you saying you don't know where he is?"

"No!"

Quinn's arms dropped to his sides. He let out a noise that

sounded like a muffled groan. Clara grabbed his arm as he started to turn away. "You wait just a minute, Quinn Cavanaugh! You tell me what's going on. What's happened?"

He stopped; his body halfway turned away from her. "Benjie wasn't in his room this morning. I thought you might know where he's gone. I thought maybe that ex-wife of mine had come back to town and that he was with her."

"No," said Clara. "Becky's in Tennessee. I just got back from going out there to see her. You sit down and tell me what's going on. Why do you think Benjie's missing?"

Quinn stumbled more than sat down in a chair beside one of the tables. He rubbed a hand across his eyes. "We had an argument last night," he said. "I made him go to his room, but when I got up this morning, he was gone. The bed wasn't slept in."

"And you thought I'd kidnapped him? Or that Becky had?" Clara's voice had risen. She looked over at the table, where everyone was frankly staring avidly at them. "Do you honestly think I'd do something like that, Quinn? Do you?" she repeated in a lower voice.

"No," he admitted. "But I'm out of my mind with worry. I've been looking everywhere I can think of for him."

"You said you had an argument last night. What was the argument about?"

"It was something totally stupid," Quinn admitted. "Benjie wanted to go over to Billy's house to play those silly video games that they sit for hours staring at. But I asked him if he'd finished his science project, and he said no. So, I told him that he couldn't go to Billy's until his schoolwork was finished, and we argued. I sent him to his room."

"Did you check with Billy's folks? Is he there?"

"That's the first place I looked. They hadn't seen him. I've been driving around everywhere I thought he might be, looking for him."

Just then there came a ringing sound from a pouch Quinn had attached to his belt. He unsnapped it and pulled out a cell phone. "It's Donna," he said, clicking it on. "What's happening?" he said into the phone and listened for a full minute as Clara stood beside him. "Okay," he said at last. "Yeah, you're right. Okay." He slid the instrument back into his pouch and looked up at Clara. "That was Donna. Benjie showed up at school this morning. He's all right."

"Thank God!" said Clara. "Where was he?"

"Seems like he slipped out his bedroom window with his sleeping bag and spent the night in the woods," Quinn told her. "Then he just walked to school this morning like nothing had happened."

Clara couldn't suppress a slight smile.

"Donna and I were both beside ourselves with worry!" Quinn burst out. "What is the matter with that boy?"

"He's fourteen years old," Clara said. "That's the main thing that's wrong with him."

"Well, when I get my hands on him ..." murmured Quinn.

"You ought to wait until he gets home from school today to deal with this," said Clara. "You'll all have clearer heads by then."

"You sound like my wife," said Quinn. "That's just exactly what Donna said."

"She's a smart lady."

"Yeah. Look, Clara, about what I said earlier ..."

Clara put her hand on Quinn's shoulder. "You were worried and upset. But I do want to make something very clear to you. None of us ... not me, not my sister, *nobody* would do anything that would cause you a minute's worry. I hope you realize that."

Quinn averted his eyes. "Yeah, I know that, Clara. I'm sorry. I don't think that even Becky would just come and take Benjie away."

"No, she wouldn't," Clara said firmly.

"I'm sorry."

"You were scared. I understand that," said Clara. "Believe me, I do know how you feel about that boy."

Quinn got to his feet. "Thanks, Clara."

"Quinn," she said softly as he started to walk away. He turned back to her. "Go easy on him, okay? He's your boy … and you know how many stunts you pulled when you were his age that gave *your* mama gray hairs. He wouldn't be your son—or Becky's—if he was some meek little thing that never showed any spirit. So, remember that, okay?"

Quinn allowed himself a slight grin. "You're right, Clara. But I *will* deal with it. Bye now."

"Bye, Quinn," she said and turned back toward her customers, who were looking everywhere except in her direction, pretending that they hadn't heard a word.

Chapter Eighteen

Clara was reclining on her old sofa, leafing through a magazine, her TV tuned to a sitcom she wasn't really watching, when her telephone rang.

"Now, who's that bothering me tonight?" she murmured as she went into the hallway to pick up the call. "Hello? Oh, hello, Donna. How you doin'? Is everything all right?" She listened for a moment, and a smile slowly spread over her face.

"On Friday afternoon? Yeah, Al will let me have the time off if I ask him … I'd love to come to Benjie's graduation. Thank you for asking me. I can't believe that boy's old enough to be finishing up the eighth grade and going to high school next year. I know." She listened.

"Okay. Thank you again for asking me to come. One thirty on Friday in the school auditorium. I'll be more than happy to sit with you. I just appreciate your thinking of me to include me. Yes, I know I'm his aunt, and I want you to know that I do appreciate being included. See you on Friday. Bye." Clara was smiling when she returned to the living room to sit back down.

On Friday afternoon, Clara made her way through the little crowd of people at the back of the auditorium at Phillips Elementary

School. Her eyes roved over the sparsely filled rows of seats that made up the three sections, separated by two wide aisles leading up to the stage in front of the building; the heavy velvet curtains were now pulled closed. Several rows at the front of the middle section were empty and roped off by ribbons at either end of the rows, evidently reserved for the graduates.

Suddenly, she spotted Donna, who was looking backward over her shoulder and sitting in the center section, not too far behind the reserved section. Donna caught Clara's eye and waved. Clara made her way down the aisle toward her.

The row's first two seats were empty, and sitting just beyond Donna were little Sammy and Amy Lynne, and in the seat just beyond the little girl was Quinn's mother, her back ramrod straight. She was trying to control the squirming toddler.

Donna smiled. "Have a seat," she said, greeting Clara. "We're still waiting for Quinn to show up; he's coming over here from work."

"Hello, Donna," said Clara, sitting down. She caught Donna's mother-in-law's eye. "Hello, Mrs. Cavanaugh. How are you?"

The woman gave her a tight-lipped smile and nod, and reached forward and down to retrieve Amy Lynne, who was trying to crawl under the seat in front of her.

"Hi, Sammy," said Clara, smiling at him across his mother. The little boy smiled and ducked his head, his big, brown eyes solemn as he looked back at her.

The auditorium was filling. Moments later, Quinn made his way across the row of seats toward them. He gave Clara a quick smile and a nod of greeting. "Let me get in between them," he said to Donna, squeezing in front of them. They all shifted seats, and he sat down in the seat between his children.

"Divide and conquer," Donna whispered to Clara. "I brought the camera," she told Quinn.

"Good," he said approvingly, giving her a warm smile.

A woman walked across the front of the room and took her place at the upright piano beside the steps leading up to one side of the stage. Someone adjusted the lights, and the woman began pounding out "Pomp and Circumstance" on the piano. The audience quieted.

Twin lines of eighth graders marched down the aisle on either side of the middle section of seats toward the section reserved for them at the front. Taking alternate rows, they filed in solemnly. Most of the young girls wore white dresses, and the boys wore dark slacks, button-down shirts, and ties. Scattered through the lines were some who wore more casual attire, but all of them carried themselves proudly as they marched to their places.

The principal moved to the lectern at the center of the stage and greeted everyone, after which one of the local ministers went up front and offered a prayer. Then one of the students made her way forward, climbed up the steps to the stage, and took her place behind the lectern. She began addressing the assemblage in a firm, clear voice.

"That's Pamela Clarkson," whispered Donna. "She's the vale-dictorian of the class. She's the daughter of the principal over at West High School."

When the girl finished her speech to polite applause from her classmates and the audience, another girl, all long, coltish arms and legs in her frilly, white dress, made her way across the stage and took her place behind the lectern. She began speaking, looking out across the audience with sparkling eyes and punctuating her remarks with a few relaxed, graceful gestures of her hands. When she concluded her speech, her classmates applauded wildly; some-one whistled, and a voice yelled, "Yo, Katy!"

"That was Katy Burgess," whispered Donna. "She's the salu-tatorian. I had her in my first-grade class."

"Everyone seems to like her," Clara whispered back.

"Oh, yes! Sweet girl. Very popular. She's a natural leader."

The principal returned to center stage, accompanied by one of the teachers. The first row of graduates rose and marched to the side steps of the stage. The teacher began calling out the names of the graduates, and they began filing quickly across the stage to accept the rolled-up diplomas. The second row rose and filed forward, and one by one, each name was announced, and the smiling eighth grader went forward to shake the principal's hand and receive his or her diploma.

"I'm so glad they do this," Donna whispered. "Some of them will drop out of school before they finish high school, and this will be the only graduation they will ever have. At least they'll have this to remember."

Just then Benjie's name was called, and Clara joined in the family applause as he shook hands with his principal and took his diploma.

At the ceremony's end, Clara filed out with the Cavanaughs, and they found Benjie outside, where he and other graduates were milling around, laughing, and talking to their relatives and classmates. Donna snapped several pictures of him alone and with his family members before they all joined the crowd gathering in the school lunchroom for fruit punch and cookies to celebrate the occasion.

"I'll give you copies of my pictures," Donna told Clara as they sipped the sweet, fruity drinks.

"Thank you," said Clara. "I do appreciate your including me."

"Well, you should be included!" retorted Donna. "You're family, too."

"I'd like to send a copy of some of the photos to my sister," said Clara.

Donna hesitated for only half a heartbeat. "Sure," she said casually. "I'll give you extra copies of the ones she'd like."

Becky counted the rings until finally someone picked up the telephone. "Hello!" she caroled and laughed when she heard the response.

"Becky!" Clara cried happily when she heard the voice on the other end of the line. "How are you? What's going on?"

"Busy, busy, busy," Becky said. "What else is new? I guess you heard that my TV show just got renewed for next year."

"I did," said Clara. "Congratulations."

"A-aa-nd," said Becky, "I just made a new record album."

"Really? What's it about?"

"Oh, the usual," said Becky with a laugh. "An unhappy woman with a pint of Jack Daniel's, a pickup truck, and a pair of pink cowgirl boots on a quest for revenge."

Clara laughed in return. "Is it doing good?"

"Yes, it actually is. That's what I'm calling about. Tripp and I are on a promo trip. I'm making stops in several cities on a swing through the south. We'll be in Charlotte next Wednesday."

"Oh, really?"

"Yeah. Got a live guest appearance with one of the DJs on a local country radio show, and—get this—I'm going to be at the opening of a big car dealership. They're getting TV coverage, having a grand opening with refreshments, prizes, and meet Becky Barnes, star of ... yada yada."

"Sounds like fun," said Clara.

"No, it really isn't," said Becky. "It's a lot of hard work, but it's good publicity for both the show and my new album. So, we're doing it. Then it's on to Richmond, Virginia, on Friday morning and something there. Don't remember exactly what. That's Tripp's job; he keeps up with all that stuff. But the reason I called is, I thought maybe we could swing by and see you while we're so close by. It's only an hour and a quarter's drive up there from Charlotte while on our way to Richmond. We could rent a car and come by on Wednesday night. That is, if you want us to."

"Of course, I do!"

"Good! I was hoping you would. Oh, and Clara."

"What?"

"Do you think there's any chance that I could maybe get to see Benjie, too?"

"I don't know," said Clara. "I can ask."

"Thanks, sis." Becky's voice grew more subdued. "I'd really like to see him."

"You got the pictures I sent you? Of his graduation?"

"I sure did! They were so good. I can't tell you how much I appreciate—"

"Thank Donna," said Clara.

"I know. She's been wonderful."

"I'll talk to her. Maybe she can bring him over here on Wednesday night."

"Thanks, sis. We'll see you next Wednesday evening."

Chapter Nineteen

"How's my favorite almost sister?" Tripp's voice boomed as he wrapped his long arms around Clara and swung her off her feet when she answered their knock on Wednesday evening.

"Fine! I'm good," she said, laughing as he put her down. She turned to Becky, who came sweeping in right behind him to give her a big hug. "You look so pretty!"

"What a day! What an incredibly long, exhausting day," said Becky. "But we're finally here, where it's so nice and quiet, and we can relax for a few hours."

"You love it." Tripp grinned at her. "She thrives on all this," he told Clara. "She claims she can't hardly stand it and complains about how bad she needs a break, but she'd be tired of all this peace and quiet you got here within a week."

"I know it," Clara replied. "Are you guys hungry? I've got food on the table in the kitchen—chicken, potatoes, some salad ..."

"Oh, God! Sounds like heaven! I'm starving," cried Becky, and they trooped through the house to the kitchen to fill their plates.

"Did you get hold of Donna?" asked Becky after they had finished eating, stacked their plates in the sink, and moved back into the living room.

Clara nodded. "I did. She said that she and Benjie would come by for a little while. They'll be here about eight o'clock, she said."

"Oh, thank you, Clara! You're the best," said Becky, settling back into one of the two armchairs.

"You been watching Becky's show?" asked Tripp, sitting down in the other chair.

"Every week," Clara assured him, taking her place on the sofa.

"What do you think of it?" he persisted.

"Well," said Clara, "it does get a little risqué sometimes. But I just love the episodes where Becky gets to sing."

"The risqué stuff is what keeps the ratings up," said Tripp.

"Not my singing?" Becky said quickly.

"That, too," Tripp said, smiling at her. "You know they wouldn't even have a show without that."

"Looks like Donna's here," Clara said, eyeing the window. "I saw the light from a pair of headlights turning off the street and up my driveway."

There was the sound of car doors slamming shut outside. The three of them fell silent as Clara rose to her feet to go to the front door.

Clara pulled open the door, switching on the porchlight. Donna and Benjie were crossing the porch. Following them up the porch steps into the light was a tall, imposing, masculine figure.

Clara pushed open the screen door. "Hello, Donna. Hello, Benjie," she said with a welcoming smile. "Hello, Quinn. It's been a long time since you've been to this house."

Quinn inclined his head. "Clara," he said. "Yes, it has. I guess I haven't been here since your mother died. Am I still welcome?"

"Of course, you are. Come in. All of you come in," said Clara.

They moved past her into the house. Becky rose to her feet, a huge smile lighting her face as Benjie entered the living room, but she froze in place when she caught sight of her ex-husband walking in behind Donna.

"I need to get us another chair." Clara scurried down to the kitchen and brought back one of the ladder-back chairs from the table there, maneuvering it into the entrance of the small room, which suddenly seemed full of people.

As silence fell over the room, Tripp stood up and extended his hand toward Quinn. "I don't think the two of us have ever actually met," he said in his gravelly voice. "I'm Tripp Thomas."

Quinn's icy-blue eyes swept over him, and the heavy silence in the room seemed to intensify. No one appeared to breathe as Tripp stood there, arm extended, and the two men locked eyes for what seemed like a very long time. Finally, slowly, Quinn's arm rose from his side, and the two clasped hands briefly. "Quinn Cavanaugh," he said.

"Everybody, let's all sit down," Clara said in a soft voice. "Can I get anything to drink for anybody? Glass of sweet tea?"

There were a couple of headshakes, and the recent arrivals settled themselves onto the sofa, while Clara pulled her chair a little farther into the room and sank down onto it. Becky and Tripp settled back down into their armchairs.

Becky cleared her throat. "How have you been, Benjie?" she asked, beaming a smile his way.

"Fine," he mumbled, not meeting her eyes.

"How are you, Becky?" ventured Donna. "I understand you're traveling around, promoting your new record. Is that right?"

"Yes, I am," she replied. "There's a song on it we introduced a few weeks ago on my TV show. Did you happen to catch it?"

Donna shook her head just as Quinn firmly said, "No."

"I did," Clara said into the new silence. "I watch you every week."

"Well, we're working on promotions. That's what we're doing right now," Tripp said. "We're going around to some of the major cities in this area to promote her new album on some of the radio shows during this free time we've got before we start taping next season's shows. I guess you heard that the show got renewed for next year."

"Congratulations," said Donna. "We did hear that."

"I was hoping Benjie might be able to come visit us in Nashville sometime," Becky said wistfully, looking at him. "You could come on the set and watch us shoot one of the episodes from behind the scenes. You'd like that, wouldn't you, Benjie?"

"Cool!" said Benjie, cutting his eyes in a quick glance at her.

"You have seen your mama's show, haven't you, Benjie?" Tripp asked him.

Benjie nodded just as Quinn said, "We don't watch it at our house." Quinn looked at Benjie sharply. "Where did you see it? Not at the house."

Benjie looked down at his lap. "I watched it over at Billy's one night," he mumbled.

Quinn raised his eyebrows. "Oh, really?"

Benjie squirmed.

"We don't think your show is suitable viewing for young children," Quinn said, looking directly at Becky. "We don't watch it at our house."

"I don't think it's as bad as all that," Becky replied. Her voice sounded defensive.

"It does get a little bit explicit in some of its content," Donna said. "We just prefer that our children watch shows that are a little more wholesome until they're older."

"Evidently, Benjie doesn't agree with that." Tripp grinned.

"Evidently." Quinn sounded grim.

"He was probably curious about it," Clara said, trying to smooth things over. "He knew it was Becky's show. He probably wanted to watch her in it and see what it was all about."

"It's not like it's X-rated or something," Becky said.

"Of course not," said Donna. "We just think some of the scenes are a little too sexually explicit for the children to see. Sammy and Amy Lynne are too young."

Benjie continued to sit between Donna and Quinn, looking extremely uncomfortable.

"Uh, Benjie," said Becky, attempting to change the subject, "have you learned to drive your Pinto yet?"

"Of course I can. But Daddy won't let me drive it anywhere until I'm sixteen."

"You have to get your license first," said Donna.

"But I can drive it," Benjie told her earnestly. "I take it around the yard every so often, so the battery won't die."

"You can handle it okay? Even though it's a straight shift?" asked Becky.

Benjie shrugged. "That's not a problem. Straight shifts aren't hard."

Becky smiled. "Good for you. It won't be long until you can get your license."

Another silence fell across the room.

"So," exclaimed Becky, breaking it, "you're going to be in high school next year, Benjie! Before you know it, you'll be out of school and ready to go off somewhere to college. Have you thought about where you want to go yet?"

"No," he replied. "I don't think I want to go to college anyway."

"Oh, really? Why not?" Becky asked him.

"I don't need to go to college to do what I want to do."

"What do you want to do? Do you already know?"

Benjie looked at her. "Yes. I want to fly airplanes. I'm going to be a pilot when I get out of school. I don't need to go to college to do that."

"Are you sure about that?" Quinn chuckled.

"I'm pretty sure."

"Well, I wouldn't bet on it," his father told him, smiling

indulgently. "They probably will require a college degree by the time you get ready to do that."

"Don't you want to go to work with your father in his business?" asked Becky.

"No. I want to fly." He looked at Quinn. "Sammy can be the one to help you in the business when he grows up. He likes that stuff. But you know that I've always wanted to be a pilot."

"So you've always said," Quinn agreed.

"Well, what I was getting at," Becky said. "Benjie, when you get ready to go off to college, maybe I can help you out. Now that my show's a success ... well, I want to help you pay your college tuition."

"I'm perfectly capable of taking care of my son's college," Quinn said stiffly.

"I know you are," Becky said quickly. "But he's my son, too, and I want to do this."

"No!"

"Why not?" cried Becky. "I just want to have a little part in Benjie's life." She looked at Quinn, whose face was like cold granite as he looked at her with those icy-blue eyes. Donna opened her mouth as though to speak but remained silent, reached over, and simply slipped her hand into Quinn's.

"Why do you keep trying to block me? Why don't you want to let me have any part of Benjie's life?"

Quinn leaned forward, color rising on his face. "Because you ran off and left him behind! You made that decision a long time ago!"

Becky and Quinn glared at each other. After a moment, tears sprang into her eyes, and her face crumpled. "I'm sorry," she whispered. "Quinn, I'm so sorry I hurt you. The way I left ... that was wrong." She looked entreatingly at him. "I didn't mean to hurt you," she repeated. "But you and I..." Her gaze dropped to Benjie, and she chose her words carefully as she looked back up at Quinn. "We ... didn't have a forever kind of situation. You know that!" She shook her head and implored him with her eyes. "I'm so sorry I did it like that. Can you ever forgive me ... just a little bit?"

Quinn kept looking stoically at her, but his expression softened slightly.

"And you had Benjie," she added.

Quinn gave a sharp nod. "Yeah. I did. He's mine! And that's not going to change, no matter how rich and famous you get!"

"Whoa, whoa." Tripp held up a placating hand. "Let's not get too far off the track here. Becky, I believe that you just wanted to ask Benjie to come out to visit us. Isn't that so? Maybe he could come out with his Aunt Clara here, if that might suit his folks." He looked back and forth between Becky and the Cavanaughs. "Or maybe all of you might like to stop by. We'd be mighty glad to have you. Got room to put all of you up for the night. What do you say?"

"Doubt that's going to happen," muttered Quinn.

"Clara," Tripp said jovially, "tell them—you've been out to see us. We got us a nice place. You'd be glad to bring Benjie with you, both of you could come out to spend a weekend with us, couldn't you?"

"Sure. I sure could," Clara said, looking at Donna and Quinn.

"How about it, Benjie?" asked Tripp. "How'd you like to fly out to Nashville with Aunt Clara, see the sights, watch us, and see how a TV show is made? Maybe you could take a ride through town in one of those horse-drawn carriage rides they got for the tourists while you're there. You'd like that, wouldn't you?"

"Sure," said Benjie.

"Look," Tripp said, gazing earnestly at Donna and Quinn. "That's all we're asking. Just a little visit or two from time to time to give Becky and Benjie a chance to get acquainted. What do you say?"

"We'll think about it," Donna said finally, breaking a long silence.

"Wouldn't it be great if Benjie could come to see us when we get home from this promotion tour? Then he could be there when I have my interview with *People* magazine," commented Becky.

"What interview with *People* magazine?" asked Clara. Tripp was frowning at Becky.

"Oh," said Becky, stretching her arms above her head and smiling smugly. "*People* magazine is scheduled to do an article on me in a couple of weeks—right after we start shooting again for our second season. They want to do an in-depth article about how I transitioned over from just doing country music singing in clubs and making records to getting the lead on my TV show, where I don't just sing—I do acting *and* singing. Then they want to cover how much that's helped my career, how it's made me a national household name now, not just a country singer in Nashville. They're going to do a photo spread and everything and talk about how Tripp and I have been together for so long and how he's my partner and manager. Isn't that just the coolest thing ever?"

"And you think it'd be a good idea to have Benjie there for that?" Quinn asked, the quiet whisper of his voice belying the sharp look he sent her.

"No," said Tripp. "I don't think so, Becky."

Becky looked at him with a puzzled expression.

"Just how were you planning to introduce Benjie to this reporter, Becky?" Quinn asked softly. "Were you going to announce that Benjie is your son?"

"No," she said. "I mean ... no, of course not."

Quinn shook his head. "I will not have you use my son for a publicity stunt. That's not going to happen. Not ever."

"I wasn't—"

"Yes, you would! You'd do anything to promote yourself without giving a single thought to the consequences. Well, you can forget about it. I won't let you use Benjie, then just toss him aside again like a broken toy when he's served his purpose whenever it suits you."

"I'd never do anything like that!" Becky cried. "Why, I've never even said where I came from—that I'm from Phillips, North Carolina—in my publicity. Nobody knows exactly where Becky Barnes even came from."

"That's probably going to change," said Tripp.

"What do you mean?"

"Becky," Tripp said patiently, "I'm the one who's put out all your publicity in the past. Your publicity has said exactly what I wanted it to say, because I've had to pay for every word of it, so I've had total control over what was out there. Even in the interviews you used to give, back when you were just singing and making records. I screened the questions they asked you. That's going to be changing real soon now."

"Why?"

"You're becoming a bigger star now. The public is going to want to know all about you. The reporters are going to ask all kinds of questions, look for stories to print. We're going to have to be real careful about everything we tell them."

"Oh," said Becky. "I guess you're right."

"And you sure as hell ain't going to be telling anybody that you've got a fourteen-year-old son back in Phillips, North Carolina," said Tripp. "Not that there's anything wrong with it, of course."

"No. I won't do that."

"You sure as hell better not," said Quinn through gritted teeth.

"Of course, I won't," said Becky. "I just wasn't thinking a minute ago when I said that."

"How long do you think it'll take them to dig it out?" asked Quinn. "Once they start digging into her past, find out what her real name is and where she's from."

"Not long, assuming that they do that," Tripp said. "But it's not going to happen—not right now. This is just going to be a little puff piece about Becky Barnes's rise to fame. I'm the one who will be giving them the background for their story. For right now I'm not even going to let them know her name used to be Becky Smith. It'll be all right for now as long as she stays under the radar and doesn't get herself mixed up in a scandal or something. We just have to make sure she stays out of the tabloids."

"You sure about that?" asked Quinn.

"Yeah," said Tripp. "I'm pretty sure."

"Make sure you keep it that way," growled Quinn.

Tripp nodded. "I will. And if you let Benjie come out to visit us, all anybody is going to know is that he's an old friend of the family. I'll promise you that, and you can hold me to it."

"Clara, too?" asked Quinn. "What if somebody finds out what her name is and that she's Becky's sister?"

"Clara, too," said Tripp. "Nobody needs to know who she is. It's nobody's business. It will be a quiet visit, without a word to the media."

Quinn stared at him for a while, then nodded.

"Great!" Tripp slapped his hand against his thigh. "Well, Becky, are you about ready to head out? We've got to drive back down to Charlotte. We've got a plane to catch in the morning."

"I thought you were going to spend the night here," protested Clara.

"Nah, I think it might be best if we head on out. We'll let you all think about what we've talked about." He stood and extended his hand, palm up, toward Becky. "Are you ready, hon?"

Becky looked back and forth between Tripp and Clara. "I guess so," she said. She stood. "I'll just go get my things."

"I wish you would stay," said Clara, getting to her feet.

Tripp walked over and put his arm around her. He gave her a kiss on the cheek. "A good showman always knows when to leave the stage," he whispered into her ear. Becky came back into the room with her purse, and the two sisters embraced.

"I'll see you soon," Becky said.

Clara nodded. "I wish you would stay the night. You could drive to Virginia in the morning when you're all rested up."

Becky and Tripp exchanged a look. "All right," Becky conceded, and they sat back down.

"I guess we ought to be going, too," Quinn said as Clara walked back to her chair.

"No, stay and visit awhile," said Clara. "It's been so long."

Quinn gave her a rueful smile. "I know, Clara. I guess I haven't been real nice to you over the years, and you've never been anything but good to me—and Benjie. I guess I was holding Becky's actions against all of you." He avoided looking at his ex-wife.

"I can see how you might do that," Clara said, sneaking a look at Becky, who didn't react.

"Still doesn't make it right."

"Don't worry about it, Quinn. Let's just leave it in the past. Let me get you all a glass of tea or something. Surely you can stay long enough for that."

"Well, all right," said Donna. She looked at her husband. "We can stay long enough to have a glass of tea."

He smiled at her and gave a tiny nod. Donna got up. "Here, Clara, I'll help you." The two women walked out to the kitchen, leaving Quinn and Benjie sitting side by side on the sofa, along with Becky and Tripp in their chairs.

"Do you think Becky is going to splash Benjie across the pages of a magazine or get a story about him in one of those trashy tabloid papers?" Donna asked as they put ice cubes into four glasses.

"No," said Clara firmly. "She knows better. She wouldn't do that."

"Not even accidentally?"

"No." Clara paused, pouring liquid into the glasses. "Becky's a smart woman. She knows better than to do something that would ruin her relationship with Benjie the way that would."

"Are you sure?"

Clara nodded. "She really wants to get to know Benjie—to have him in her life. She won't do anything that would keep that from happening."

"I hope you're right," said Donna. They carried a tray with the glasses of cold tea into the living room.

"What have you been doing this summer, Benjie?" Becky asked as they sipped.

"I've been helping my dad," he replied.

"Is that right? Good for you," said Clara, raising her eyebrows.

"Yeah, I've been giving him a few things to do," said Quinn. "He's old enough to work a little bit."

"Do you like the excavation business?" asked Clara.

"No," Benjie replied.

Quinn chuckled. "He's telling the truth. All he wants to do is go up and fly the plane."

"I told you. I want to be a pilot. I want to fly every day."

"He loves it," Donna murmured. "He definitely has his opinions about things."

"Hmm," said Clara. "Maybe we should ask Benjie what he thinks about all this, since he has his opinions on things."

"Opinion on what?" asked Quinn.

"Benjie," said Clara. "How do you feel about going out to visit Becky? What do you think of her?"

A small frown creased his forehead. "I dunno. She seems like a nice lady, I guess." Benjie looked at Becky and gave her a little grin. Becky smiled back at him warmly.

"Do you want to go to see her at her home out in Nashville? She's your birth mother, you know," persisted Clara.

"I wouldn't mind it, I guess," Benjie said, his chin coming up as he looked Clara straight in the eye. "But she's not my mom—you know that. Donna's my mom."

Donna's face lit up, and a small smile lifted the corners of Quinn's mouth. Clara smiled at Benjie. "You're a pretty smart boy. You know that, Benjie? We all know that you don't really know Becky very well. I just wanted to know how you felt about going to visit her and, you know, getting to know her better. I think she really wants that."

Benjie took a deep breath. "I guess that a visit would be all right. I'd like to see what's out there; I've never seen Nashville." He raised one shoulder in a half shrug. "They seem nice enough, Tripp and Becky, I mean. I guess it would be fun to go see you if you want me to," Benjie finished, looking straight at them.

"Thank you, Benjie," Clara said solemnly. "I appreciate your opinion on this matter." She looked at his parents. "Now, I think we all feel better about this whole thing. I'd be more than happy to go out there with him on a visit if that meets with your approval."

"As long as it doesn't turn into a publicity stunt," said Quinn. "I don't want his picture plastered across the tabloids or a bunch of reporters and photographers showing up here in Phillips, hounding us." Quinn gave Tripp a hard look.

"I don't think that will happen," said Tripp. "I think we can keep it from ever happening."

"What do you think, Donna?" asked Quinn.

"I think it will be all right as long as Becky and Tripp promise they'll do everything in their power to keep it away from the press."

"Oh, yes, we will!" promised Becky, and Tripp nodded emphatically.

"I think they will," said Clara. "Becky knows it's in her best interest to do that."

"Then I guess it won't hurt anything if he goes out there with you for a few days," said Quinn. "Becky has to pay for the tickets, though."

"I'll be glad to!" Becky cried.

"Well, we'd better be getting on home then. Are you about ready, Donna? We have to stop by my mom's house and pick up our two little ones on the way home."

"Bring them over here one day soon. All of you can come see me," said Clara.

"We'll do that," Donna promised.

"Bye, Benjie. Looks like you and I are going to be taking us a trip together later this summer," said Clara as they all walked toward the door. Becky and Tripp exchanged a high five behind their backs as the group left the room.

"Good." Quinn gave her a small smile. He paused at the door and hugged Clara before he went out.

"Make sure you schedule the trip to take place after she's had that interview with *People* magazine," cautioned Quinn, looking back over his shoulder as they crossed the yard toward their car.

"Oh, yes! I'll make sure of that," said Clara. "Bye, everybody."

After she closed the door behind them, Clara leaned against her front door and closed her eyes for a moment. She went back into the living room, where Tripp and Becky were doing a silent gig of jubilation. They reached out and drew her into their happy dance.

"Can you believe this?" Becky caroled when they stopped for breath.

"Oh, yeah! Benjie and I will be coming to visit you in Nashville!"

"Becky's got a new hit, the show got renewed, and she's a national star both as a singer and as an actress!" Tripp added.

"And we're all family again." Becky laughed. "Well, at least Quinn can be in the same room with me."

Clara gave a little laugh.

Tripp took Becky into his arms. "Happy?" he asked.

She hugged him back. "Oh, yes, I am. What more could I ask for?"

If you loved *Glitter*, then you won't want to miss *Warrior*, the next in Eliza Grace Howard's series. It's coming soon!

Gina Thompson, born and raised in Phillips, has always had a deep fascination with anything to do with the American Indian, even though she has never even met one. So just out of school and in her first job at Terri's Interiors in Winston-Salem, she is thrilled when her boss, Terri Green, asks Gina to accompany her on a buying trip to Albuquerque and Santa Fe, New Mexico, for south-western items for her business.

Gina uses a break in her work to explore the Indian Cultural Center in Albuquerque. While there, she meets Jerrod, a handsome Pueblo. She learns that he is an out-of-work carpenter and that work is almost nonexistent due to the current economy there. She makes the offhanded comment that her uncle back in North Carolina owns a construction company and is always looking for good employees.

To Gina's surprise and delight, a few days after her return, Jerrod turns up at her door, having taken the long bus trip to North Carolina, hoping to find a job. Uncle Hugh hires him, but as time passes and their friendship begins to blossom, unexpected attitudes and obstacles begin to appear in the sleepy, little town. Can Gina and Jerrod overcome these heretofore hidden prejudices and build a life together?

Also available is *Choice*, the first story in the series, available at Elizagracehoward.com or wherever you buy books.

Donna Porter is a married first-grade teacher with a domineering husband, Stanley. Against her wishes, he forces her into the swinger lifestyle. Donna is miserable with this arrangement but feels powerless to say no to her husband's desires. Following an abusive encounter, she has no choice but to flee.

Away from her husband and in the process of getting a divorce, Donna begins a relationship with Quinn Cavanaugh, the father of one of her students. Quinn is virile, charismatic, and very appealing. He shows her the love and respect that's missing from her marriage, but they can't ride off into the sunset with a happily ever after just yet.

Stanley threatens to reveal details that could jeopardize Donna's career and reputation in their small, conservative southern town. The dread hanging over her head complicates Donna's relationship with Quinn. Can she get through this divorce unscathed, and if so, can Quinn protect her from the past?

Printed in the USA
CPSIA information can be obtained
at www.ICGtesting.com
LVHW080817311023
762205LV00010B/363/J